THE BUCK STOPS

Sean Seebach

This is a work of fiction. Names, characters, organizations, places, events, and incidents are either products of the author's imagination or used fictitiously. Any resemblance of actual persons, living or dead, or actual events is purely coincidental. But seriously, if you or someone you know are aware of an actual were-deer, please contact the authorities.

No product of this work may be reproduced, or stored in a retrieval system, or transmitted in any form or by any means, electronic, mechanical, photocopying, recording, or otherwise, without written permission of the publisher.

Copyright © 2020 Sean Seebach
Cover Design: Elderlemon Design
Editor: B. Wagner

ISBN-13: 9798646007453

THE BUCK STOPS HERE

SEAN SEEBACH

ACKNOWLEDGEMENT

A special thanks to authors Alan Baxter and Kealan Patrick Burke (who also designed the killer cover!) for getting writers writing about animals native to their home state started on Twitter. All proceeds from The Buck Stops Here will benefit the World Wildlife Federation.

And a huge thank you to you, the reader, for supporting this cause. I hope you enjoy this one. Any errors are mine, as always.

For Koro

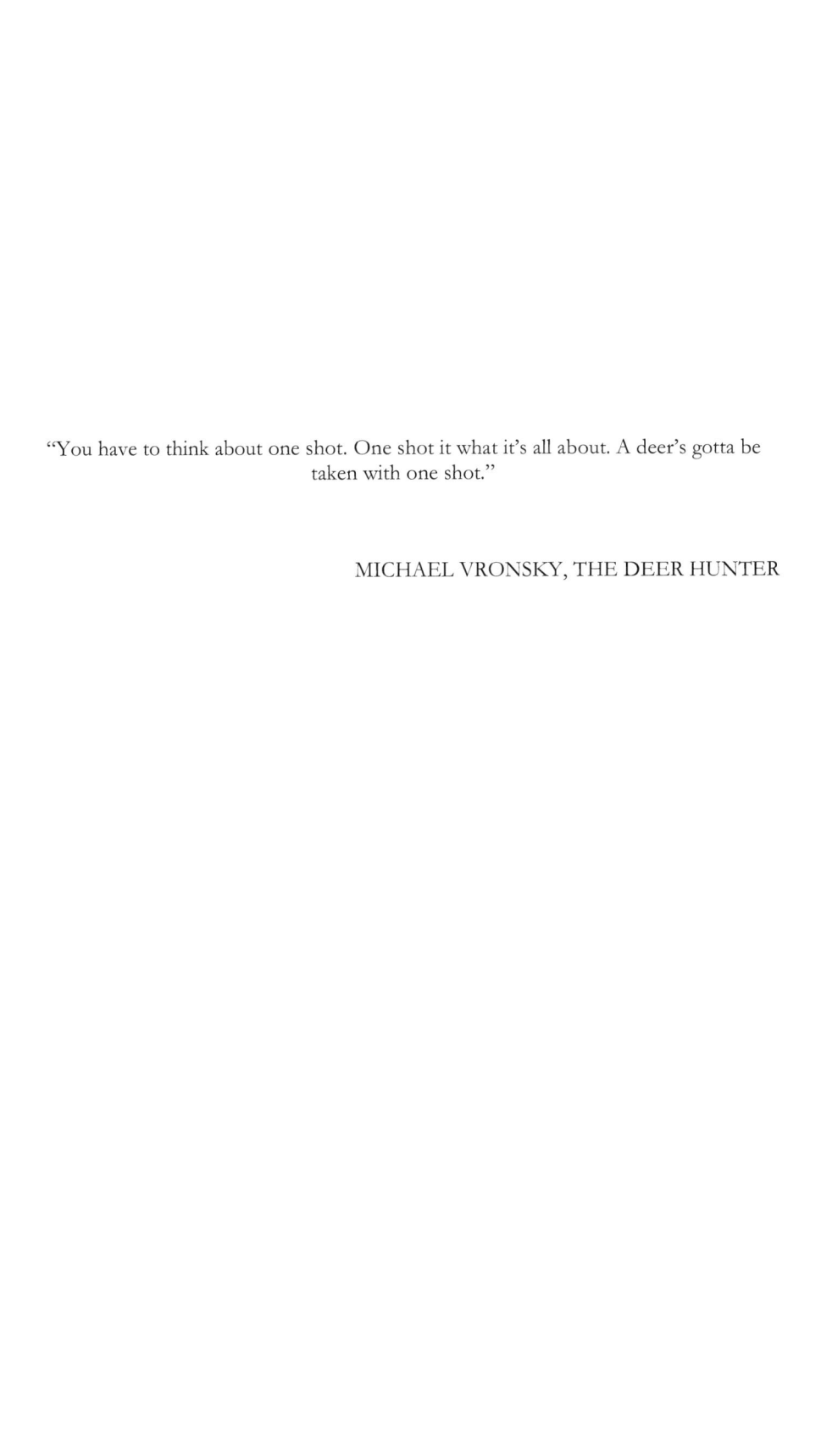

"You have to think about one shot. One shot it what it's all about. A deer's gotta be taken with one shot."

MICHAEL VRONSKY, THE DEER HUNTER

Chapter 1

By the time Caleb's tires on his BMX had found County Road 10, the autumn wind had already assaulted his face and dried his tears. With a swipe of his arm he smeared the snot dripping from his nose across his cheek, ignoring the itch from the flaky mucous already plastered to his face. He found the dampness between his legs more concerning.

How could he literally have pitched a tent in his pants while kissing Casey? He had practiced so many times with his pillow, and when the time had come where she pulled him around the corner of the house away from everyone else, he had inhaled the scent of her cherry blossom body splash, tinged with the ripe aroma of burning leaves from the neighbor's burn barrel, and parted his lips. He hadn't noticed his erection until she stepped away, when Grant and Travis and Vanessa and Holly and a few others had begun pointing at him.

Except for Casey. She hadn't laughed. Tears of embarrassment, like the ones Caleb just shed, ran down her face before she covered it with her hands and ran inside.

Caleb was never partial to Travis and was clueless as to what Grant saw in him. Sure, Travis was popular in school, but other than having an affinity for finding the most outrageous car crashes on the internet, Travis did not offer much to their social circle. He didn't like to explore the woods like Grant did, and only rode his bike with them if it involved daring jumps over garbage bins. He did date Vanessa though, which was probably the only reason Grant invited him in the first place. Quite simply, Vanessa was Travis' "in" to their tribe.

And because Casey was best friends with Vanessa and Holly, she was at Grant's, and she had told them she liked Caleb a few days prior. So, Caleb went to Grant's while his parents had gone out with some friends, even though he had never believed Vanessa or Holly. He had no reason to. They were both at the hub of the junior high rumor mill. Plus, Casey was one of the prettiest girls in school. He had a feeling she was only after a job at his father's grocery store.

But Casey must have had the hots for him in the end, at least, enough to slip her tongue into his mouth, confirming the truth behind the rumor.

Despite all his shame, guilt continued panging Caleb for choosing to spend the evening at his best friend's house instead of with his dad, who no doubt had a huge bowl of popcorn on his lap while watching a marathon of The Twilight Zone.

Caleb wondered if losing his virginity would bring the same unease as his first kiss. He doubted he would even enjoy the creature feature tonight, alone in his room now that he had been completely humiliated.

No way could he face his father.

"Why you home, son?"

"Oh, you know, got a boner in front of everyone."

Their covered mouths while pointing at the bulge in his jeans had embedded in the forefront of his mind. Wait, had they seen the wet spot too or did he orgasm after he climbed onto his BMX?

The tears came rushing back. He was thankful the moon was high and bright. Its glow bathed the road just enough to keep his face cloaked in the dark while he sped home.

Only one vehicle had passed him. He had turned his face away from the headlights, concealing his chagrin. He was pretty sure he had taken care of the boner; he had tucked the tip into the waistband of his underwear, already too small for his skinny frame, hoping it would shrink back to normal, praying the driver of the car didn't notice it.

Puberty. What a bitch. He had outgrown the undies over the summer and was just too lazy to ask his dad to hop online and order him a new pack. That would be the first thing he would do tomorrow.

He blinked hard. A quarter of a mile separated Caleb from home. Almost there. He would probably stare at his ceiling trying to forget tonight and battle the anxiety leading up to Monday morning when he would see everyone at school. Luckily, no one who witnessed the horrible blunder was in his first period class. Health, of all subjects. To boot, sex ed. was on the docket to be studied.

His hands began to shake and suddenly the trees began swaying, and out the corner of his eye came a flash followed by a smell reminding him of the time he accidentally left a pound of hamburger sitting out in the garage after removing it from the deep freeze. He couldn't remember what had seized his attention and made him forget to bring the meat inside to thaw—probably a notification ding on his phone—but he remembered what it smelled like when he found it two days later, laying in a puddle of dark liquid.

The smell enveloping him now? It was worse than that. More terrible than the tuna his dad had used in the meal helper instead of the hamburger that night. Eyes watery, Caleb squeezed the brake handle, slowing the BMX before skidding it to a full stop. A tiny burst of gravel dust clouded around his rear tire as he lowered his weight and dry heaved. The smell so strong he tasted it.

Not only did he swallow the stink, he felt the presence of who or what it belonged to behind him.

Caleb turned his head while branches from the woods swayed from the gust of a westerly wind. He did not catch a hint of autumn in his next breath, only the odor of a filthy animal who had been eating from a dumpster struck him.

He scrunched his nose and rapidly blinked, trying to clear his sight. Two red orbs flickered about the darkness at the edge of the woods up ahead.

Was it too late in the season for fireflies, he wondered? Caleb dug his face into his flannel sleeve, rubbing his eyes into the fabric. When he lowered his arm, something slashed at his face, so close he felt the wake of it cut the air. It wasn't until he felt something tickling his neck that he realized half of his face dangling against his shoulder.

Hot pain permeated from his ear clear down to his neck. His eyes rolled in their sockets and he couldn't be sure if the sky could hold the many stars he saw up there gleaming upon him. The sky turned over then, as another blow tore through the air and this time, Caleb saw it. It appeared to be a hoof attached to a skinny arm littered with fine coarse hairs. He felt only a numbing sensation around his neck before the woods flipped upside down, then right side up, over and over again.

Caleb willed his eyes shut to stop the world from spinning but before he could even try everything slowed on a tilt before finally settling askew.

And if anyone wanted to kiss Caleb Welsh again, they would find his head some thirty feet away from his BMX on the cold, dark pea gravel of county road 10.

Chapter 2

Sheriff Abigail Laine sipped black coffee from her mug while gazing out the kitchen window, remembering how well a cigarette went with morning coffee. The fog didn't help. It only reminded her of days when she did smoke, a throw speckled with southwestern motifs draping over her shoulders, blowing out thick streams of wonderful nicotine, preparing her mind for the day.

The fog hung low above a hazy mist and all she wanted to do was light up before hitting the couch to read Alan Baxter's latest, The Roo. Instead, she fumbled for the blister pack of nicotine gum on the counter with her free hand, keeping her gauge locked on the woods beyond her backyard. Her tranquility had to last before she found herself elbow deep in paperwork from last night's arrest, which should have been completed after she slammed the cell door closed. She decided it could wait. Baxter's books were that good. It wouldn't be the first time his stories had pulled her from her responsibilities. And it wasn't like Hobbes Oliver had never been arrested for drunk and disorderly either. He had practically made the cell his second home.

She chomped on the gum a few times then stuck it between her cheek and gum, just as the instructions said and waited for the flavor of damp ash to coat her tongue before she spit into the sink. Swallowing hard, she wondered why cigarettes tasted so much better than the gum—even the name brand stuff had a sooty flavor—and let the burn sting her throat before spitting the entire piece at the kitchen drain.

Determined to sink back into a place of Zen, Laine took a deep breath and steadied her shoulders, mentally falling back into a peaceful state when her phone buzzed. She nearly dropped the mug from the sound, but her first two fingers curled around the handle before it toppled, though not before most of the coffee escaped onto the kitchen linoleum.

"Yeah?"

"Abigail…um…you g-g-gotta come see this…"

She had never heard her deputy, Chuck Edwards, stammer before.

"You didn't let Squirrel talk you out of keeping him, did you?"

He blew out a breath. "No, but…just get here soon as you can."

"Where's here?" Laine unwound a few sheets of paper towels, balled them up, and mopped up the spill with her neck and shoulder pinching the phone.

"County road ten, just before the Fun Center."

"What is it, Chuck?"

"It's bad. Real bad."

"Okay. Just be cool. I'll be there in five."

He immediately ended the call.

#

Laine headed to the bathroom to brush her teeth for the second time that morning when a scream roared through her closed kitchen window.

Miss Adley. Wonder what it is this time. Mothman? Sasquatch? Another group of little green men marching single file?

Laine overturned the mug and placed it into the sink, dropped the wadded-up towels into the trash, and double checked the coffee maker to make sure it was off.

Forgot to rinse it!

Within ten seconds the coffee pot was washed out, its reservoir tilted open to allow the water to evaporate. She felt for her holster next, then ran her hands across her belt, ensuring her gear was in the correct place as she walked to the hook where her keys hung. Before she left, she took a third glance at the coffee maker. It was fine.

#

Outside, fog crept around Laine's ranch and wrapped around the tires of her cruiser. A sharp chill stabbed at her neck and, for a moment, she wished she didn't have to put her hair up for her shift. She shimmied her shoulders and rounded the rear of the cruiser, over to Miss Adley's house next door.

Miss Adley shuffled around the rear corner of her home, a baby blue double wide—the only one on their street—trampling over the plastic windmills flanking her garden.

"Abigail! Did you see him? I know you have your coffee every morning in the kitchen, you had to have seen him, indecent as the day he was born, he was, without the innocence of being a newborn, fleeing the scene like he'd done something he wasn't supposed to."

Adley jogged well for someone well into their retirement age and was quite nimble; she nearly leaped onto Laine's driveway. Laine supposed she would live to be a hundred the way she took care of herself, so long as pneumonia didn't claim her first, for Adley was still in her night gown, the same one she wore when she changed Laine's tire last month. Laine was on the road in five minutes flat.

"Seen who, Miss Adley?"

Adley rolled her eyes. "The naked man. In your backyard!"

"Are you sure it was a man?"

Adley's eyes widened as she leaned forward, held up her hand, and erected her pointer finger before wiggling it.

Laine smirked. "Okay. So it was a man. Any other description?"

"No. He was holding a branch in front of his, you know." She made that crooked finger tremor a second time. "Leaves covered part of it."

Not wanting to humor Miss Adley's claim of having witnessed yet another Weekly World News headline, while knowing she needed to get to her deputy Chuck Edwards, Laine thought it important to listen to her. Chuck's call already had her mind reeling, so had spilling the coffee. So far, this was far from a typical morning, aside from ensuring her kitchen was in order before she left.

"Hair color?"

"Dark."

"Brown, black?"

"Dunno. He ran fast, lunging with every step, like he had springboards attached to his feet."

"His bare feet."

"That's right. Why aren't you taking notes?"

Laine poked her own temple. Adley furrowed her brow.

"Well, Miss Adley, I got an urgent call. How about I come over after my shift and we can talk. Meanwhile, write down everything you saw while it's still fresh in your mind. It'll help when filling out the police report."

Adley gasped, eyes gleaming. She had reported many sightings to Laine over the ten plus years they had been neighbors, but never once had she ever taken any of them seriously enough to file a police report. "You mean it?"

"Absolutely."

Adley nodded, shifting her gaze to the woods. "Not sure I feel safe here anymore. I hear things out there at night…"

Laine opened the driver's side door of her cruiser. "Put it in your notes. We'll get to the bottom of it."

Adley hurried to the wooden stoop of her trailer and turned just before Laine had closed the door. "It was the biggest one I'd ever seen."

Laine cocked her head.

Adley wiggled her finger.

Chapter 3

When Laine arrived at the scene, Chuck Edwards had already set up a roadblock. Behind a row of orange cones sat his cruiser, strobing their lights, still effective while the sun rose. Laine noticed the cones before she noticed Chuck. She took a moment to straighten them up before she approached him. Thankfully, he hadn't secured the scene yet with bright yellow police tape. Chuck never stretched the tape across in a nice, solid line. She could never think clearly until it was right.

Chuck stood twenty yards away with his arms crossed. He chewed on a knuckle, just gazing off in the distance. Laine approached him as he shook his head and removed the knuckle from his lip, only to bring it back up again.

"Okay, Chuckles, what do you got for me?"

Without acknowledging his sheriff, Chuck Edwards simply pointed at the ground before shifting from her view.

Squinting, Laine leaned her head forward. This had to be a joke, what with it being October and all. Had to be, no way could it be real. Not here in their quiet little town of Rockbridge; *especially* quiet with summer leaving faster than the supposed naked man had from her backyard. Most of the cabins at Hocking Hills were vacant come September.

Two steps brought her closer to what was sure to be a gag, a prank, something well executed by a group of teens bored out of their minds.

Gasping, Laine reeled back. She closed her eyes after a moment but only saw Caleb Welsh's head staring back at her with half his face missing. "Can't be real."

"It's definitely real. I'm so sorry, Abigail. Body's over there."

She barely registered Chuck's voice, let alone the magnitude of the discovery. The cruiser's lights washed over her eyelids. She felt the heat emanating from Chuck's cruiser's engine as she sunk to her knees, eyes still closed. "How?"

"That's what I've been trying to crack since before I called."

"Why?"

"Dunno. I don't know who could even—"

She raised an open hand. "I don't expect an answer. I'm just…"

"Trying to process it. Yeah, me too."

She took a deep breath and never wanted a cigarette more in her life. How could she leave the package of nicotine gum on the counter? She could have stomached the flavor. It wasn't nearly as bad as how she felt.

"What am I going to tell Nick?"

At this, Chuck said nothing. He let her sort herself out loud, something she had always done. He had just been too jarred to allow her earlier and forgot when he ended the call.

The wildest thing she had ever found during her tenure in Rockbridge was catching the occasional car on a trail in the woods, windows foggy from heavy breathing inside. Sometimes, Squirrel would relieve himself in public, and even then, she wasn't as disturbed, or shocked, as she was now. This wasn't supposed to happen in Rockbridge. Then again, decapitations weren't supposed to happen anywhere.

She hoisted herself up by leaning on Chuck's patrol car and used a tremoring hand to grip the spotlight protruding above the sideview mirror. Adley's naked man was miles away from her now. All Laine could do was find the stoicism she swore she would keep when she first became an officer. But small town policing had a way of dulling the edge.

You are okay. Just pretend it's not Caleb.

She panned her vision from the dirt road to Chuck's shiny black boots, then followed the gravel to where Caleb's, no not Caleb's (he was dead), *the* head lay. The image remained out of focus for a beat, then her gauge shifted directly upon it.

Oh my god it's Caleb Welsh's head. Definitely his. Just breathe. Breathe.

Laine removed her tape recorder, the size of a vape pen, and spoke into it.

"Ahem. Um, um." She put it away. This was not an autopsy. This was her boyfriend's son.

"Look at me, Chuck."

When Chuck turned his head, she paced over to him as if the gravel were hot burning coals and embraced him.

"Who else knows about this?"

"No one. I was on my way to my spot to clock morning traffic when I saw it."

"Call Steven immediately. Get Caleb out of here before Michael catches wind. People will already be asking why the road's closed." She pulled away from him then and squeezed his shoulders. "If Michael sees this…it'll only make our jobs harder."

"We need suspects, Laine. We need a motive. We need—"

"We need to secure the area better and get samples."

"Forensics."

"We are forensics. I know its Dominque's day off but get him down here to direct traffic. He can take over for you when he gets here."

Chuck simply nodded and removed his cell. Normally, he would put up a fight for being placed on traffic duty.

Laine would have to find a new routine in the mornings. She didn't think she would ever be able to peacefully look at the woods again.

Chapter 4

Using her tablet, Laine took pictures of the crime scene first. She used the panoramic feature to get the thirty-foot trail of blood connecting Caleb's head to his body. When she snapped a photo of the BMX, she imagined an axe swiping the air and cleaving through Caleb's neck, his body tipping over, leaving the rear wheel spinning. She shook the thought away. That wasn't possible; the cut wasn't clean enough.

"Yet sharp enough to sever it." Laine closed the tablet's casing and focused on the BMX, where she found a tuft of fur jutting from the rear brakes. She plucked it out with tweezers and dropped it into a clear bag before sealing it.

"Whew. Stinks. Bad."

Scrunching her nose, she pinned the baggie to her flashlight beam and brought it to her face. Coarse black hairs intertwined with the fur.

"Odd." Yet, everything about this was peculiar.

Maybe a rabid animal had attacked Caleb but that didn't explain why his head wasn't attached. Gravel crunching underfoot broke her from thought. Chuck's cologne enveloped her.

"What is it?"

"Ever see anything like this before?"

He held the baggie to his face.

"Look at the dark hairs entangled with the fur."

Chuck shrugged. "Been hunting here all my life. Don't know any deer got hair like that."

"Could be something."

"Could be anything."

Laine stood and put her hands on her hips. "Yeah. Listen, I gotta go to Nick's before he opens the store."

"Store's gonna be closed for a while, I imagine."

"Take care of this. Call me if you find anything else and when Steven gets here."

"Should we wait?"

"I got photos. Keep scouring the road. I'll get information about where Caleb was last night."

Her mind immediately shifted to what she would say to Nick. How did one deliver news like this? She pitied herself for having to find out.

Chapter 5

Abigail waved to Dominique as she passed him, ignoring his gesture for her stop. He would find out why she dragged him out of bed soon enough and would make it up to him with an extra sick day.

"Two extra," she said," no questions asked."

It pained her to only have raised a finger at him, as if to say, "in a minute", as she passed. But Dominique was a good man. He would understand.

She pulled up to Nick Welsh's house. His old Chrysler was still in the driveway. Inside, he hurried past the bay window overlooking his down sloping front yard, running late as usual.

Tears began welling in Abigail's eyes. She put her head against the steering wheel and tried to compose herself. But she knew no rules when it came to the news she was about to deliver. She shook her head in shame, shame that such a thing had happened to such a good kid.

A memory from five years ago came flooding back to her, rushing its waters over her emotions.

Caleb was seven when Abigail began seeing Nick. Their first date consisted of the three of them going on a hike at the nearby Hocking Hills, the town's only attraction aside from the Hocking livery. They walked for only half a mile or so when Caleb looked up at her with his big brown eyes and asked, "Are you gonna be my new mommy?"

Oh, the look on Nick's face! The red splashing over his cheeks, his perfect o-shaped mouth. He looked like an exact replica of Caleb, if not for Nick's close-cropped beard. Abigail had smirked, bent down low as to meet Caleb's eyes when time, at least to her, stood still. The cool autumn breeze had stopped, stilling the ochre leaves that remained on the branches.

"Only if I'm lucky," she had said, and tousled his hair.

"Yeah," Caleb had said, "sounds about right."

She and Nick smiled at each other. He had upturned his palms, utterly flabbergasted, as if to say, "I don't know where he got that!" while Caleb continued hiking, stabbing the walking stick three inches taller than him onto the trail.

Abigail and Nick held hands, following Nick's son up a winding trail. Nick squeezed her hand, she squeezed back, and both were weightless as they walked up the incline.

"Five years...almost to the day, I bet," she said, wiping her eyes, watching Nick now hurry out the front door.

Nick barely registered the cruiser with Rockbridge Sheriff printed across it in his driveway while he fumbled for his keys, losing the tumbler of coffee stuck into the crook of his arm in the process. It rolled down the driveway and that was when he glanced up and saw Abigail getting out of her car.

"Gail?"

She rushed to him and squeezed him tight. The mace can and butt of her gun pressed against his hip.

"I'm happy to see you too but I gotta open the store!" Despite his tardiness, he embraced her anyway and ran a delicate hand over her back. "What is it?"

His neck was already damp from her tears. She had closed her eyes, deeply inhaled the fresh laundry scent of his collar, hoping it would bring her a sense of comfort. But she could only picture Caleb's head rolling from a long corridor and into view. Once the head had passed, two heads came forward, then three, then a hundred. A constant stream of Caleb heads rolling and rolling and rolling...

"It's Caleb, Nick."

"What?! What about him?" Nick pulled away, moving his hands to her elbows. "Gail?" He brushed a lock of hair from her face that wasn't there.

"He's gone, Nick."

"Come again? He stayed at a friend's house last night. Grant's."

"Well, he must've left early, because Chuck found him on Country Road 10."

Nick dropped the tumbler again. The keys followed. They slipped right from his fingers as his knees buckled. Nick placed his hands on the driveway, head hanging, instantly sobbing. He stared at the driveway while he spoke.

"You're sure? You're certain it was Caleb. My Caleb. *Our* Caleb."

"I'm so sorry, Nick."

He sniffled, then finally looked her in the face. "What happened?" His expression was accusatory, as if he blamed her for his son's death.

"We're not sure. Chuck and I aren't going to sleep until we find out who did—"

"He was murdered?"

She barely nodded, yet it seemed she had been rocking her head for hours. Nick's thunderous voice had startled her. She couldn't remember him ever raising it, but this was a side of Nick she had never seen. This was a side of her *he* had never seen. She recognized this, watching his wild eyes try to comprehend the terrible news. Empathy wasn't a question. Abigail didn't have any children of her own, but Caleb was her own. At least, he and Nick had treated her like he was. She didn't have to have delivered the boy into this world to feel the impact of the loss.

Nick sat there for a moment, chest heaving, before he turned and opened his mouth. An odor of curdled milk surrounded them as a shot of brown vomit spewed forth, spraying the black tar of the driveway. It ran fast in creamy rivulets. "Oh God."

His entire body trembled. Laine imagined he would soon explode into a hundred different bloody pieces. She touched his shoulder. Nick brushed her hand away, and the macabre thought left with it.

"Help me up please, Gail."

Frowning, she offered her hands. He clutched them and brought himself up. His wan, stone face looked past her. She thought the glare could penetrate the thickest of steel.

"I gotta call Grant's parents." He turned and headed back up the drive with vomit dangling from his brown beard flecked with random white hairs.

Abigail gathered the tumbler and keys. She couldn't tell if the moment had caused the clouds to speed above her, but they certainly were dark, racing, and bulbous. No doubt they would soon burst, taking care of the mess on the driveway.

#

A blast of pine scent hit Laine when she walked inside Nick's home. She found him sitting at the dining room table, by the bay window, shadowed by the oncoming storm threatening the town. Phone in hand, he slowly blinked at the screen, as if in doing so would force Caleb to walk through the front door. "I gotta call Grant and have him open the store."

She leaned against the kitchen counter and stared at the several ounces of coffee remaining in the pot, reminding her of the black waves of grief plaguing her mind whenever she shut her eyes. A nose emerged from the surface of the coffee and she quickly set her gaze on Nick, not allowing her imagination to take hold.

"I can do that. And I'll go to the Hargroves'." She slipped onto the wooden chair across from Nick. "I'll even stop by the store, make sure Grant's okay with everything there. You need to call Faith."

Lip quivering, Nick lowered his head onto the oak table. His sniffling weighted the atmosphere, like a wet blanket had fallen from the ceiling.

"She never answers," he said. "I can't leave a message like that."

Laine stretched her hands across the table, but not before straightening the wicker napkin holder between them and grasped his wrists. "You have to try."

She heard a scampering below her. The clouds had finally opened, she noticed, peppering the bay window with thick splatters of rain. She almost looked under the table, but soon realized the sound she had heard was not from the rain, but from Nick's tears falling onto the kitchen floor.

Laine scooted the chair out and approached him, rubbing his back while he sobbed, while she stared at the rain assaulting the road. Torn between two selves, the consoling partner and the town sheriff, she chose her duty to Rockbridge in that moment. Nick needed her, but so did the town. He wouldn't have to wait for her either. She silently vowed to make herself available when he was ready. She had enough to unpack on her own, and he had his, even though she knew she carried the lighter bag.

"I'm sorry," he said, and reached for a napkin. "You're right. I gotta call Faith until I reach her."

Laine got to the napkin first, pinching a corner between her thumb and forefinger and pulling one out. The wedge of brown wicker never moved. He took it, wiped his face, and blew his nose.

"You have nothing to apologize—"

"I can't imagine what it was like for you to come here…" He bit his lower lip. "Thank you, Gail. I love you."

Nick grabbed her head and pulled her close. Laine felt his compassion, his grief, but the longer he held her the more she felt only anger.

It was time to get to work.

Chapter 6

Laine only told the Hargroves that Nick was vomiting and asked if Grant could open the store. They asked about Nick's symptoms and whether it was, in her professional opinion, something Grant could have the chance to catch, whatever Nick had.

"I certainly hope not," she had said, and that wasn't a lie either.

She did all of this after pulling away from Nick's house, waiting for Chuck to arrive once Steven brought Caleb's body to the funeral home. Steven had volunteered this ministration due to a corporate buyout of Rockbridge's local ambulance service. They no longer transported the deceased, not when they could have a potential lifesaving opportunity for their ambulances.

The wiper blades quietly shifted as she drove the cruiser, which felt like gliding a massive brick over a smooth stream, to the station. She slowed to a stop at a yellow traffic light, her arm propped against the window. She leaned her head against the glass and glanced at her rearview, where she spotted a driver banging impatient thumbs against the steering wheel, splaying open hands at the light for not turning green fast enough.

Laine sucked the inside of her cheek and ground her boot against the cruiser's floor. Her free hand squeezed the wheel. She noticed it tremoring, then took a deep breath and released it.

They don't know any better, she thought. *Let them stew and get bitched at by their boss for being late.*

Someone a few cars back blared their horn. Laine glanced up and slowly pulled forward through the intersection, not even realizing the light had finally turned green.

She passed Welsh's Market. By this time, Nick would have had the sign lit up in neon due to the overcast hiding the sun. Glowing light would have permeated through the four large front windows behind the meager rows of shopping carts. But not now. Now the store looked like it was out of business, as if a major grocery chain had dug its claws into the town and sucked the life and financial wellbeing out of Nick.

Even though the former hadn't occurred, the latter certainly had. She sighed and hit the gas.

#

Laine slammed the cruiser door closed and stood in the station's parking lot, letting the rain pelt her shirt, watching her breath plume. Gray water spilled from the down spouts running down the corners of the police station, offering a noisy distraction. Had she had the chance, she would have stood out here until the storm quieted. But procrastination was easy. Already behind, she needed to get out in front of the evil infecting Rockbridge. She let the unpleasantness of the thought linger as she sloshed inside.

"Where's my Happy Meal, sheriff? You tryin' to starve me in this cell or what?" Squirrel. Gripping the bars, he stomped like a child who had been denied ice cream. And in a way, she supposed he had. She always made him dry out for at least twelve hours each time he was arrested and had brought him a Happy Meal at some point during his lock up.

Squirrel had a rough life. He had been caught stealing from Welsh's Market a few times. Whether it was a summer sausage tucked into his belt line or a pack of hamburger buns smashed into his coat, Nick always caught him, but never pressed charges and let him keep the stolen goods. Squirrel didn't know Laine was privy to this. He had grown accustomed to her compassion.

"I'm dying in here, girl! C'mon!"

Water puddled around Laine's boots. She slipped them off and walked to her locker down the short hallway leading to receiving, which was really only a nook with a desk used to hold her and Chuck's keys whenever they entered. Squirrel's whines followed her down that hall and tapped against her shoulder while she slipped into her rain jacket. Then she slammed the locker closed, hoping the rattling of metal would give Squirrel a hint.

She snatched her boots, careful not to step in a puddle, and approached the cell.

"I'm never *girl* to you, got it?" Laine wanted to say more, so much more, and had the verbal ammo to back it all up but knew she would regret it later.

Squirrel's eyes enlarged. He backed away, feeling the venom in her tone.

"You deserve nothing. Anywhere else and you'd be in prison. Remember that."

"I'm sorry Ms. Laine, Sheriff, Ma'am."

She barely heard him as she walked behind her desk and laced up her boots. "Just sit quiet. It'll be here soon. I have a lot of work to do."

Squirrel nodded, folding his hands together and placing them on his lap, watching her with her pen. She clicked it rapidly, rocking back in her chair, staring at the yellow pad on her desk, mouthing words to herself. Every so often she would pause, begin to write something, then scratch it out.

The ripping of each wasted page echoed in the quiet chamber of Rockbridge Police Headquarters, which hadn't seen a fresh coat of paint since its inception. She glanced at the drop ceiling tiles and the water stains which twisted through them. The place always reminded her of a dungeon, regardless of how many community posters she hung up.

Her eyes flicked to Squirrel. He immediately broke eye contact with her.

"You ever see anything shady when you're out hunting?" She assumed Squirrel would fold his arms and shake his head until he ate, but he bounced once on the cot and shifted his legs toward her.

"What you mean exactly?"

"Anything out of the ordinary? Like a permanent camp or something."

"Kids go back there camping all the time when Mother Nature ain't raggin'."

"Fine choice of words, Squirrel. So, no?"

"Aw, you mean the stuff that crazy old bat Adley's always screamin' 'bout. In that case, no, I ain't seen no Bigfoot or Mothman out there in them woods. No little pale men with almond eyes neither."

Laine smirked. "Thanks."

"But I do hear things."

"Go on."

"Like, uh." He rubbed his arms, decorated with homemade tattoos so blurry they appeared as one giant sea of dull color. "Like, hissing." He put his tongue up to his teeth and mimicked what he was trying to explain. "Sometimes, sounds like a loud burp come after. And last a while too. Now, I've been huntin' in them woods since I was a pup. I know what a whitetail buck supposed to sound like." He made another funny noise, but this one was more primal and believable. "Gowre-ah-ah-ah," was what Laine put down on the pad.

"That's what they supposed to sound like. Gore-ah-ah-ah-ah—"

"Okay, okay, I get it. If you were to hear it again, could you identify it?"

"A whitetail?"

"No, the other sound. The different one."

"Hisssssss, gore-up-gore-up-hisssssss. That one?"

"Yes."

"Sure. But I can't identify it. Figured I was just hearing a deer come down with sumpthin' is all. Why? You think it's sumpthin' else?"

"I don't know. That's why I'm asking."

Squirrel placed a knobby finger to his chin. "You know, if I were to go back out there, I bet I could show you where I heard it. But it's waaaay back there, over a few hills and whatnot."

"I bet you could. You're here until noon."

"You can make a 'ception since I'm gonna help you."

"Suppose I could."

Chuck burst in and shimmied his shoulders, flinging water like a German Shepherd fresh from a swim. "Could what?"

Laine nearly fell from her chair Chuck had swooped in so fast.

"Could get out and help you guys," Squirrel said.

Chuck rolled his eyes and half smirked. "Okaaaay."

"I was just asking Squirrel if he ever heard anything strange in the woods. Oh, and thanks for the heart attack."

"Sorry, it's really coming down now."

A crack followed Chuck's pronouncement, and the lights cut out.

"Noooo," Squirrel said, as if they were in a movie theater and the screen had gone black.

Soon, a low rumble came from outside, and the lights flickered back on.

"I'm surprised that old generator still runs." Chuck removed his jacket and sat on the chair across from Laine's desk. He rolled up to it and chewed his thumbnail. "Scene's cleared and secured. Told Dominique to stay put."

"Is he mad?"

"Not in the least bit. He's happy you called."

"I knew he'd be."

Squirrel stood and gripped the bars imprisoning him. "What's going on out there?"

"Oh, it's just God bowling, Squirrel," Chuck said. "He always bowls three hundred, so it'll be a while before you stop hearing the pins crash."

"Ha, ha, very funny. Ya know what I mean."

Chuck spit a piece of thumbnail out. "It's nunya, Squirrel. As in, none of ya business."

"Already is my business. Sheriff needs my help."

Chuck held a hand to his mouth. "We need to release him so we can discuss this."

Laine knew it. Squirrel couldn't keep his mouth shut, but neither could anyone else in Rockbridge. "We're gonna drop you off and come back later to get you, sound good? I might even decide to waive your last three arrests if you can stay sober between now and then."

She hadn't even logged his last five arrests.

"Oh, you can count on me, Sheriff. Don't that make me a citizen's arrestor or sumpthin'?"

"No, it means you have information that could lead to an arrest," Chuck said. "It's called cooperating with the police."

Squirrel slightly frowned at this news. Laine glared at Chuck, whose dad was worse off than Squirrel. He had drunk so much in his long life his nose had turned the color of a beet, which was ironic because he was a farmer. His drinking never resulted in violence, but he was the lowest of the low when it came to deadbeat dads, always choosing a bottle over a pair of new shoes for his only child who grew to be six foot three. She knew where Chuck's disdain for Squirrel derived from, but she also knew Chuck's awareness of Squirrel's innocuous intentions.

"We'll give you a citizen's badge, how's that?" Laine said.

Squirrel smiled, showing his teeth.

Chuck leaned in. "Do we even have those?"

"Came in two days ago. What, opening packages below your paygrade?"

Chuck eased back. Squirrel stuck his chest out a little. Of course, Laine didn't have a citizen's badge. She made that up on the spot. But it brightened up Squirrel a little and if he could uphold his part of the deal, maybe he could lead them to something.

Chapter 7

Squirrel chewed with his mouth open, always left his cell smelling like an unwashed armpit, and, in a new discovery, liked to cluck his tongue while he rode in a car. Laine couldn't help but smile at these qualities while Chuck sulked next to her. If she was being honest, Squirrel had helped shift her mind more to the case itself than to Caleb's death. For the first time since graduating from the academy, Laine felt like a true cop.

She pulled up to Squirrel's place, a one-bedroom A-Frame house in the center of town, as lightning veined the sky. The house reminded her of a child's toy waiting for a massive hand to come down from above and pick it up.

She thought a gentle soul hid underneath Squirrel's scars and tattoos. His birth name was Hobbes, but Squirrel was no paper tiger. His temper had hindered his life. Maybe if she played the role of Calvin, the best version of him would come to life. All Squirrel needed was a little encouragement and some responsibility.

"We'll be back before dark," she said over her shoulder while Chuck let him out.

"I'll be ready, Sheriff," Squirrel said, squinting, scooting across the backseat. He held up the prize from his Happy Meal before he got completely out. "Race car. My nephew will love it."

Laine smiled and waited for Squirrel to finish saluting Chuck.

"That's one fine character we have," Chuck said, sliding back onto the passenger seat.

"He's harmless and you know it."

"Yeah, I guess you're right. You ready?"

Laine never answered. She sped down the road and focused on returning to the scene. "Did you find anything out there?"

"Nothing. The area was abuzz. Michael showed up wearing that stupid hat. He had an index card stuck into the band that said PRESS."

Laine snorted. "God."

"He nearly blinded me from that damn camera of his, flashing bulb and all. He thinks he's a photojournalist from the 50's or something."

"Was he—"

"Smoking a cigar? No. But he had one tucked into the side of his mouth."

"What'd you tell him?"

"I told him to get lost."

"And…"

"He stayed. But he must have a hundred close-ups of Dominique. He did a good job blocking Michael's view the entire time."

"He'll find out soon enough. I called the Hargroves. Grant is opening the store. He's going to wonder why Caleb isn't opening it for Nick."

"Damn. How'd that go?"

"I kept it short." She waved to Dominique, who had cleared the area.

He greeted her at the side of the cruiser, rainwater brimming from the bill of his hat. Dominique was smart, always prepared. Unlike her, he had worn his police issued rain jacket when he first arrived, and had the collar pulled up to his ears.

Laine got out.

"Sheriff." Dominique nodded; his hands shoved deep in his pockets.

"Dominique. Thank you. You get two extra sick days for this. Just make sure you use them before the year's up."

"That's not necessary."

She gave him a look that could force a wolf to cower. "Go home. It's your day off."

"I'm here for whatever you need."

"I know. The next few days, and weeks, will be hell for all of us. Go, dry off, turn your phone off before I call you back out here in this mess."

"You might wanna come with me first." Dominique turned on a dime and sloshed toward the tree line of the woods. "Found something here while waiting for you. Surprised Chuck missed it."

She glanced over at Chuck, to see if he had heard Dominique, but Chuck was wrestling with his jacket, trying to get the zipper up. Dominique removed his flashlight from his pocket and bathed the woods in a wide glow. She followed the light up a small embankment as thunder cracked the atmosphere.

"Two-eighty," Chuck said behind her.

She gave a wry smile but didn't need to. Her pause was enough. "You're still on that bowling quip?" Then she looked away. Chuck was being Chuck, always filtering dread with humor.

"Right here," Dominique said after hoisting himself up onto the top of the embankment and parting from where his beam locked. "They're pretty deep. Not sure what kind of deer could leave tracks like this, but one did."

Laine got down on her knees. The prints were the size of her fists. She removed her phone and captured the image. "That is deep."

"What is it?" A cloud of Chuck's breath evaporated over her shoulder.

"You ever see a deer large enough to leave an indentation this big?"

He leaned forward, narrowing his eyes. "That's not from a deer. Couldn't be."

"Then what left it?"

Chuck studied it for a moment before picking up a nearby stick and poking at the great groove in the mud as if in doing so would force the imprint to tell its deepest and darkest secrets. "A buffalo maybe, but not a deer."

"It was a stampede!" Laine stood, flicked orange and red leaves from her shins, and removed her flashlight. She swept the area in light while needles of water struck through its beam. "There's another one."

She and Dominique inched forward. "Dominique, keep your light in front of me." She snapped another photo. "Where're the other two?"

"Other two what?" Chuck grabbed a low hanging branch and lifted himself up to join them.

"Hoof prints. There're only two, as if the deer"—she turned to Chuck, "or buffalo, was preying on its hind legs."

"Deer don't attack people," Dominique said.

"And we don't have buffalo roaming Ohio."

"Maybe one escaped The Wilds?" Chuck said.

"I was there last summer. They don't have buffalo there." Laine then gripped her chin and went a little further past her two officers.

They were able to cover more ground now that she and Dominique both had their flashlights out. The prints gradually grew fainter the further they lay due to the rain collecting inside of them. Laine picked up a stick and batted away foliage and leaves. The sky lit up, and in that instant the entire forest brightened, then went almost full dark again.

Laine wiped her nose on her sleeve. "Figures we get a downpour."

She kept at it though, poking around with the stick. Soon Dominique did the same, ruffling debris around where Laine thought the hoof prints would logically lead, but that proved futile—a great gust of wind blew and nearly knocked them both over. Laine lowered herself with one arm raised. The rain increased, darting from the east in rapid fire succession. Only the left side of her pants were soaked, and she already felt her leg beginning to sting.

Laine sighed and lifted the beam, inspecting tree trunks and neighboring brush for clues when the sound of a horn blared nearby, followed by tires screeching and metal colliding.

Her shoulders slumped. She turned around. Chuck was already headed to his patrol car. His mouth moved, but she could not decipher his words. It was pointless trying to talk in this weather. She nearly slid on her rear trying to get to him.

"I'll handle it," he said, his words clearer now that he faced her. "This thing is important to me, to all of us, but I know how important it is to you." Chuck patted her shoulder. "Probably just a fender bender anyway. Take Dominique back and we'll scour these woods, if that's okay with you. We'll build a raft if we have to."

"Radio me immediately when you get to the scene."

Chuck nodded.

"I supposed we all better get," she said as Dominique joined them. "Searching the woods during this storm is pointless anyway."

Chapter 8

Laine drove to Welsh's Market. She thought about hitting the flashers and parking right outside the entrance but did not want to bring unnecessary attention to herself. No need to spark people's questions.

Laine shuddered when she pushed the entrance door open. Grant stood at the only checkout lane, swiping packages of toilet paper, loaves of bread, and gallons of milk by the fistful.

What unusual precautions people take, Laine thought, *when a storm hits*. She approached the Customer Service Center, obviously closed, and grabbed the wet floor sign leaning against the desk. Watery shoe prints laced with black grime littered the tile past the rubber mat. She placed the sign down in the middle of them, then straightened the sign evenly before marching toward the aisle keeping the coffee.

"Wet enough for ya, Sheriff?" Bill Richards said. He was Rockbridge's only plumber and he spoke while cradling a package of toilet paper. He wore a yellow rain slicker over denim overalls and in that moment all Laine could think about was shoving down his inverted pockets.

Laine smiled. "Not quite yet. Give it another inch or two, Bill."

Bill placed the toilet tissue into the cart's child seat and went to push his cart forward. "Say, is County 10 still blocked off?"

"It is. Until further notice. We'll just have to travel through town to get to the main drag until it's ready."

"What happened?"

In Laine's peripheral, she spotted Jenn Acton within earshot, reaching for a six-pack of iced coffee. Jenn had turned her head ever so slightly and tuned her ear to their conversation.

"Confidential, Bill."

Bill flashed perfectly squared dentures. His eyes met Jenn, then went back to Laine. "You know what I heard? I heard someone OD'd on some pills out there last night. Is it true? Was there a dead body?"

Caleb's head flashed in Laine's mind. She dropped the bag of ground Arabica in her hand, but swiftly bent over and grabbed it. "Don't you have some milk to buy or a basement to unflood?"

"They's sold out." Bill slightly grinned, showing Laine he knew he had hit a nerve.

"Look," Laine said. "I'll let you in on a little secret." She held her breath so she wouldn't have to smell the wafting stench of Copenhagen coming from Bill's mouth, then raised a hand to her own mouth in case Jenn could read lips. "I think Miss Adley is on to something."

"Get out! Really?"

Laine shrugged, and headed for the line where impatient shoppers stared at tabloid magazines. No one noticed her. Not that she was surprised. She lived in a world where video streaming had taken the place of social interaction, killing the camaraderie amongst the people it infected. No one even decorated their homes for the seasons anymore. No red, white, and blue during the Fourth of July, no scarecrows or pumpkins donning porches for Halloween. The only lights strung for Christmas happened to be in the establishment she now stood in.

When she finally handed the coffee to Grant, she worried he would feel the oily residue on the bag from her sweaty hand. But he looked drained. Pink rims circled his lazy eyes which were unable to focus on anything except the mindless chore of scanning items.

"That'll be four sixty-two, Sheriff."

Laine shoved her card into the card reader.

"Cash back?"

"No thanks."

"Do you think Caleb's got what Nick has?"

"I dunno. He was at your house last night. How'd he look?"

Grant looked away. "He, um, looked fine I guess."

"Nick's working on getting someone in here to cover the evening shift," Laine said. "Mind if we talk later?"

Grant swallowed hard. "Yeah, that'd be okay I guess. Am I in trouble?"

She had his attention. "Not in the least bit. I'll be by at four."

Grant nodded.

"Thanks."

"Um, want, like, a bag? It's raining pretty hard out there."

"I'm good. See ya soon."

Laine booked it to the cruiser, happy she only had to answer to Bill. However, she needed to change clothes. The stinging sensation on her leg had turned to a massive itch and her bladder throbbed.

She glanced inside the store before pulling away. Grant looked at the cruiser through the window a few times while scanning groceries. If it weren't for Nick's need to have Grant cover the store, she already would've questioned him. She hoped the rain would last until someone could cover for him. Then she could offer him a ride home without it looking like an arrest. He knew something.

Chapter 9

After relieving herself, Laine went into her closet and removed a fresh pair of pants from a hanger. She peeled the damp pants off, dried her leg, and then applied skin cream to the reddened areas. With the fresh pants on she fell on her bed. Her alarm clock read a quarter to eleven. Dark shadows pulled across her bedroom, making it feel like 10:45pm instead of am.

She had experienced every emotion except for joy, and it wasn't even lunch time yet. Her sorrow had been wrenched out of her. She had been squeezed of every teardrop. Sleep began wrapping its tendrils through her mind, pulling her away from the horror of the morning. It felt good to close her eyes. All she needed was a power nap and a good cup of hot coffee to get herself back in the game. The storm had washed away any immediate evidence. She remembered streams of rainwater running over the tarred and pea graveled road. If there were tire marks, they were long gone by the time she had arrived. And Chuck would've certainly seen them.

Then again, he had missed the hoof prints Dominique found.

Dominique had kept himself and his family out of the town's affairs. He had moved to Rockbridge only three months ago. He didn't frequent The Hill, Rockbridge's only bar, like most of the town did. In fact, the only time Laine recalled ever seeing him out with his family was for the end of summer bash at Edward's Escape in Hocking Hills. Dominique could treat the case without personal affection, which Laine hoped would provide clarity in finding Caleb's killer.

Chuck was still useful, of course, but had not been as sharp as Dominique. She wondered what else he may have missed.

Laine pulled her knees to her chest, pulled the blanket her sister had knitted for her around her shoulders. Fifteen minutes wouldn't hurt, plenty of time for Chuck to rejoin her so they could scour the woods until Grant got off work. Besides, he was to call her after he was done with the fender bender. And still she needed to find someone to cover for Grant. By that time though, she suspected Michael would already have something up on his blog, a news source much of Rockbridge unfortunately took as gospel.

Outside, rain continued pelting her house, lulling her to sleep. Her eyelids slowly rose, then fell. The blackout curtains over her bedroom window hid the flashes of lightning. Rumbling thunder only relaxed her as she drifted.

Somewhere under the eye of this storm lay the nexus of a brutally murdered boy, impossible animal tracks, and an unknown killer.

Chapter 10

Squirrel ripped the race car from the package and set it on his desk, which was only his dining room table. He went straight for the fridge and opened it. A left over tv dinner and three beers stared back at him between half a bottle of ketchup and a block of pepper jack cheese. He opened the crisper and pulled out jerky made from the deer he had harvested last winter before closing the door.

The ignored beer seemed to speak to him as he walked to the dining room table, but he ignored it and the saliva rushing from the rear of his mouth. Squirrel didn't understand this as addiction, simply as a craving, and if he wanted to turn things around, he had better start now. The sheriff had thrown down the gauntlet and gave him a challenge not to drink until she arrived. Elation immediately filled him at the trust she had put in him.

He knew exactly where he would take her too. His tree stand had stood a quarter mile into the woods, out a little ways from Nick's place. That was where he heard the sick deer, or what he had rationalized the sounds as. Maybe it was something else though. A wolf or even a bear, but he didn't think so. He had searched the web for weird animal sounds after he returned from hunting that day and only came up with hits about a supposed dog man which had been sighted in the 90's. Squirrel would've liked to have believed in such a creature, but in the thousands of hours he had spent in the woods, he figured he would've already seen something strange by now, if something like a dog man even existed in the first place. The only thing he found odd in the wilderness was the hush of the woods, and the notion it gave him that he was the last person on earth whenever he was in them.

He ripped a chunk of jerky off and chewed, firing up the old pc his sister had given him in spring. She had used her tax return to get his nephew, Jericho, a laptop computer for school and had no need for it anymore, claiming the laptop was both of theirs. But Squirrel knew his sister. She would relinquish it all to Jericho once he continued turning in all A's.

Despite the computer's age, it still worked. He put the glasses on he had bought from Welsh's Market and with one finger typed HIGH SCHOOL GED into the search bar; he had almost swallowed the piece of jerky he had been chewing by the time he had entered all the words. He felt inspired and cozy in his tiny kitchen. What with the storm crashing around outside and rain echoing off the tin roof above him, Squirrel thought this moment was meant for him; a time he could look back on after his success and think, *yes, helping the sheriff by not drinking proved a major turning point in my life.*

And a promise was a promise, and with the new technology in his home he had told his sister he would get his GED. Really, Squirrel wanted to become a forest ranger. Tired of going out of town for temporary work, digging trenches for gas lines and running a plow from his old Ford which he wasn't legally allowed to operate anyway, Squirrel thought he would be good at sustaining maintenance at any of the state parks in Ohio. The idea of moving away didn't appeal to him, but his house would be paid off in ten years and he had enough equity in it to do so if it sold, at the right price. His father had taken him hunting his entire life, so he knew about nature's unpredictability. Squirrel also had a keen sense of direction, strong survival skills, and had been on his own once he turned seventeen.

Some people understood engines, some had perfect pitch, and others had a natural ability to lead or understand numbers, often both. Ol' Squirrel Oliver had all the qualities of a competent scout leader and thought his experiences would make him a fine forest ranger. He wasn't sure how the DUI's would affect his employment, but if he could help on the case, maybe Laine would pardon his mistakes and write him a letter of recommendation.

GED IN 30 DAYS! That link seemed like a good one, but the moment he motioned the mouse there a knock came at his front door.

He hoped it wasn't Buzz, wanting to partake in some afternoon drinking. Buzz was a real maniac, and often liked to drink late Friday nights and well into early Saturday evening so he could spend all day recovering on Sunday before the work week began.

Squirrel pushed the glasses to the crown of his head and ambled to the door, nearly choking on the next morsel of jerky.

He swung the door open and there Chuck stood with his head cloaked in a dark blue hood, dripping wet. His right hand twitched. "Mind if I come in?"

"Uh, yeah, sorry, I wasn't 'spectin' you back so soon. Where's Abigail? I mean, where's the sheriff?"

"She's waiting back at the station," Chuck said, stepping inside, not waiting for Squirrel to welcome him inside.

He brushed against Squirrel's chest, leaving a streak of wetness across his t-shirt. Without removing his rain jacket, Chuck plopped down on a cushion which had the stuffing spilling out of it. Head still bowed, he said, "I got a proposal."

"C'mon, dude, you're getting my couch all wet."

"Drink."

Squirrel stood at the front door and nudged it shut. "Come again, brother?"

"You heard me. Or are all your brain cells dead?"

"You heard the sheriff. I'm not to drink until after we scout the woods."

Chuck sat there with a puddling forming below him, hands folded in prayer against his forehead. "You're not going to make this easy on me, are you?"

"I don't understand what the big deal is. Why you want me to drink? I can't blow this opportunity for a couple of beers."

Chuck lifted his head. The hood shadowed most of his face, but Squirrel didn't need his glasses to confirm the crimson orbs floating in the darkness within the hood. Just to be sure, he dropped them to the bridge of his nose anyway. He immediately wished he hadn't.

The Buck Stops Here

A long furry snout jutted above Chuck's mouth, which stretched back as if pulleys he could not see worked the lips back. Chuck chomped at the air, working out a crick in his jaw.

Squirrel reeled into the front door. "Chuck?"

Hooves the size of rubber mallets shot forth from Chuck's rain jacket. Squirrel stepped onto the landing leading to the loft upstairs, trying to comprehend. Below the hooves grew hands covered in fine brown fur. Chuck lurched forward, knocking an ashtray and a copy of Ohio Wildlife off the coffee table which soon collapsed. Black fabric tore in great splits from his police issued pants, ripping the yellow stitching along the sides clean apart. The hooves swung back, uncovering the hood, allowing room for the ten-point rack now sprouting from Chuck's head. The rack twisted like a pretzel. Yellow tinged bone, sharpened at the ends, splintered upright from the skull and bled at the base.

Stars blurred Squirrel's vision. He fought the fainting sensation clouding his senses and scrambled up the steps. He got halfway up before cursing himself for not fleeing through the front door.

His gun locker stood in the corner of the loft and the only reason he had it was for when Jericho came to visit him. He rushed to the safe and tried to remember Jericho's birthday, but his hands trembled, and he couldn't get a firm grip on the combination lock.

From downstairs came the sound he had in the woods. Hisss-gore-up, gore-up! The nonsensical gibberish ran up the staircase and surrounded Squirrel. He covered his ears and tried to remember.

"02-02-12, 02-02-12." He was sure he had the date right, Groundhog's Day, and Blake had just turned nine, but he could not get his stupid hand to stop shaking. Finally, he gripped his wrist with his other hand, steadied it, and completed the turns right as the rain outside. A heavy thud sounded, and the door to the gun safe came ajar.

Two rifles hung in front of his crossbow. He completely ignored the bow, didn't think about the repercussions from missing the monster with the rifle, and grabbed the Tikka model which used to be his father's and loaded it with Sako cartridges. He could hit a one-inch group at one hundred yards, because to Squirrel, a humane kill was the only kill to execute. But the thing downstairs? He couldn't care less if it suffered.

He turned toward the staircase, expecting a thing straight from the fires of hell to be standing there, but only the wall stared back at him. As he crept forward, inching toward the top step, he looked for the tips of the antlers. Foot by foot, the staircase revealed itself. Each one of them vacant, except for the smell.

Squirrel shut his eyes for a moment, took a deep breath, and immediately regretted it. He had once tracked a deer he had shot with his bow when he was fifteen for hours during an unseasonably warm November and recalled the bile stench emitting from the body when he found it. The odor he now winced at smelled the same, only more sinister, purposeful, like the creature in his home was supposed to stink like this.

His eyes began to water. He drove the butt of the gun into his shoulder, slid the glasses back to the top of his head, and wiped his sweaty hands on his jeans before his foot landed on the staircase. Willing the barrel of the gun still, he descended with his back to the wall. Across from him, the wall recessed. Soon he would see the living room.

He pointed the tip of the barrel in the space where the wall ended and clicked the safety off, something he should have done first. Squirrel was a good shot, but never had he been in this type of environment with this kind of prey. It felt unnatural to him to be holding his dad's old rifle, ready to fire, in his own home, the one place where he should have felt safe. If the Chuck-thing wasn't lurking in plain sight, he would ease himself out the front door and run like hell. And if it was standing there, breathing heavy, snarling, ready to eat him, he had better not miss. Jenn Acton lived next door with her mother. There was no telling if the bullets would penetrate the walls, but no one would believe him if he tried to explain why he had shot the gun in his home in the first place, especially if he accidentally killed someone. And what if he did shoot it and it transformed back into Chuck? How many years could he get for killing an officer of the law?

Too many.

Chuck's shredded rain jacket draped over the coffee table. His boots lay underneath, still standing up. The smell was stronger down here and, combined with the already musty atmosphere from the storm, threatened a sneeze. Squirrel scrunched his nose and twisted his face, fighting it off. A single distraction could take his life. Years of patience from a tree stand during the most critical of opportunities rejected the involuntary reaction, and Squirrel had made it to the landing. Still no sign of the beast. Or of Chuck. Maybe if Squirrel was just a few inches taller, he could've reached the doorknob from here, but he would have to make it safely to the welcome mat with the silhouette of two naked women holding pistols on it to do that.

The next stepped creaked when he put his weight on it, and in that instant the monster revealed itself. Full charge, antlers lowered, from the far recesses of the open kitchen. Squirrel always hated that the utility closet was tucked away in a cubby, where the washer and dryer made too much noise for him to enjoy his favorite shows. And now he knew why: it proved to be the perfect hiding place, even for a seven-foot abnormality.

Squirrel aimed with his finger on the trigger, and mumbled something to God, but in that instant the glasses fell onto his nose. He raised the barrel too high and blasted a hole in the roof. Plaster exploded. Cocking the gun, he knew it was too late, but he tried to get another shot off anyway when the antlers pierced his chest and drove him into the wall.

The blood from Squirrel's mouth spewed like an erupting volcano, thick and flowing. He was vaguely aware of the gurgling escaping his throat as the room went blurry. A framed photo of him and Jericho holding an eight-inch largemouth fell from the wall and crashed onto the floor. The antlers went deeper. Squirrel felt himself slide toward the massive spine below him.

When the antlers lowered, a busted rib bone penetrated Squirrel's lung. Blood sprayed, and everything went dark.

The antlers bucked, arcing Squirrel's body into the air and toward the kitchen. His fingers nudged the toy from the Happy Meal for Jericho on the way down. The tiny race car rolled into the mouse, forcing the monitor out of sleep mode. There, glowing faintly on the monitor, was a site never to be visited, a link for Squirrel to enter his application to get his GED. A ticket for a new life that would never be punched.

Chapter 11

Laine stirred and finally opened her eyes. She bolted upright and glanced at the clock ticking away above her dresser. She had slept three hours.

Slipping off the mattress, she rushed to the kitchen and poured coffee into the brew basket. The filter collapsed.

"Shit." She began removing a bowl from the cupboard in order to save the grounds but was so upset with herself she dumped the coffee into the trash, rinsed the remaining grounds free, and started again.

The aroma of coffee brewing calmed her moments later as she checked her phone to no new calls. She expected at least two: one from Nick and another from Chuck. She dialed Chuck first, since Nick had plenty on his plate. The call went to voice mail.

She stared at the coffee maker. "What's taking so long?" This was more about Chuck's tardiness than the coffee maker.

Abigail shook her head while rinsing her thermos, perturbed she had fallen asleep. She would try Chuck again on her way to the market to pick up Grant.

She filled her thermos, dropped an ice cube into it, and grabbed a protein bar and braced for the storm. But the rain had slowed to a drizzle. Her breath plumed as she rounded her cruiser. She shimmied her shoulders, shaking off the chill, and fired the engine. Just as she began pulling out of her driveway, Miss Adley came running from her trailer waving her arms, notebook in hand.

"Shit. Shit."

Adley motioned her to roll down the window.

"Hey," she said, gasping and sliding the notebook into the window gap. "My statement is in there, along with a few other things. I expect what's inside there stays between us?"

"Of course, Miss Adley. Sorry I didn't come over sooner."

"You've been home for a few hours?"

"Yeah…not feeling too hot. Needed to rest before I went back out."

"Have you ate?"

Laine raised the protein bar. "Got this, thanks. I gotta get going."

"Oh. Well, I wrote my number at the top of the first page in case you need me to clarify anything."

Laine gently pulled the cruiser further, but Adley ran out into the road. Laine pulled half the cruiser into her lawn and rolled the window completely down. The elderly woman chewed her bottom lip. Laine thought it was the only the rain beading her face, but now that she had a real good look at her, she realized sweat had coated the woman's brow.

"I gotta tell you something that I didn't jot down." Adley glanced down the road, both ways, then whispered while Laine's left leg vibrated, silently trying to get the woman on her way. "I tried to write it down, I really did, but I just couldn't do it. My hand wouldn't allow me."

Laine lifted a brow.

"Remember the naked man I told you I saw in your backyard?"

"How could I forget, Miss Adley?"

"Well, gosh it makes me sick to my stomach to even say it…it looked an awful lot like Nick Welsh."

Laine put the cruiser in park. "Come again?"

Adley showed a worried smile. "I know, I know, I'm sure it wasn't him but gosh it did look an awful lot like him. Gray stubble and all." She waved her hands around her head. "Wavy hair, about 5'10". Scrawny."

Laine sighed. "Thank you. I'll keep that in mind." She put the cruiser in drive and tapped the gas, not allowing Adley to dive onto the trunk or throw herself in the way.

She's lost it, Laine thought while glancing at her in the rearview mirror. Adley looked as if she regretted the accusation as soon as it left her mouth, and still did. She had her arms folded in a T as if contemplating something important.

Miss Adley shrank in the rearview until Laine made a left into town. It felt good to get her out of sight, even if she had lost something. Something being either her mind or medication, but that was insulting. Truth was, Laine didn't know much about Adley. Sure, she made preposterous claims about things she had seen which could make Weekly World News headlines, but she was nice to Abigail, and lonely, and probably just wanted some company. Apparently, Abigail didn't know a whole lot about the people in Rockbridge or even Nick. She missed the call that he would be streaking in the middle of the night on the eve of his son's death.

She pulled over. Did Adley know about Caleb already? Keeping it secret was only driving her anxiety. She had fallen asleep when she should've been scouring the murder scene. The image of her straightening up the wet floor sign when she entered Welsh's market flashed in her mind. Her sister had made her aware that she had awful OCD and that was the only reason she and Nick hadn't yet moved in together.

I'm using it as a coping mechanism, that's all. True, and this situation called for a head clear of distractions.

When she arrived at Welsh's Market, the parking lot was empty. Sorry We're Closed donned the double glass doors underneath a handwritten note taped to the door: *Out of power, closed until further notice.* A sharp pain twisted her stomach. Cleary the market had power. The faint glow from the cold cuts case burned in the back of the store. She could see it from her cruiser.

Chapter 12

Chuck awoke on the floor of Hobbes Oliver's home in a bloody mess. His head pounded, worse than it had the last time the fury took hold. He didn't realize his feet were bare until he stood.

I did it again. Squirrel lay ten feet in front of him, chest cavity splayed open as if the guy had been underneath a jackhammer, emitting a stench of raw meat.

Inside the dimly lit house, Chuck tapped the top of his own head before laying his hands fully upon it. He searched the kitchen cabinet, moved the various bottles of hot sauce to one side and found a bottle of aspirin. He chewed three, then stuck his mouth under the faucet. Minutes passed before he finished drinking.

No use in getting the body out unnoticed. Squirrel bled like a stuck pig. Chuck moved the kitchen curtain aside and peered out the window, wondering if anyone had heard and was snooping around. His fingers brushed away from the doily fabric. The curtain fluttered back in place.

Chuck had walked here from the station. He had thought that through. But his clothes were shredded. The notion of needing to change them once the fury arrived hadn't dawned on him though. Nobody knew he was here. At least he had that going for him.

He stepped over the blood blossoming on the carpet. Something crunched underfoot. "Son-of-a-bitch!" Shards of plaster and nails littered the floor. He narrowed his eyes and glanced up at the hole blown into the ceiling.

"Shit."

Over by the front door lay a rifle. He glanced over at Squirrel, eyes permanently wide. "Always were a fucking pain in the ass, weren't ya?"

All the smart ass left him though when a knock came at the door. Chuck's heart pounded harder than the anticipation of the fury. And the door had no peephole. He side-stepped to the bottom staircase, fully aware of his large frame making the floor squeak. Two steps up and he had saw the top of Jennifer Acton's head through the door's transom window. Her red flowing curls were unmistakable.

She heard the shot go off.

He cleared his throat and cracked the door, allowing only his face to show through the gap between the door and the jamb. "Hey, Jenn. Official police business here. I must ask you to leave. Don't worry. I have the place secure."

She was texting and a beat passed before she even acknowledged him. "Um, you sure? Because that bang was *loud*. Is Squirrel okay?"

"We're all good here. Have a nice day." Chuck slammed the door and locked it before she had the chance to see his face. He pressed his back against the door, waiting for the feeling of her presence to vacate the porch.

Got lucky she didn't look up. Last time the antlers weren't even all the way gone.

Chuck coughed, then turned around and lifted himself upon his toes, watching Jenn amble off the porch, still looking at her phone. He waited until she was completely gone before he inched toward the kitchen, looking for his socks. They lay in the utility room, for some reason, along with his rain jacket and deputy shirt.

Always in stealth mode, atta-boy, Chuck!

Faced with two options, he needed to save the atta-boys until he got himself out of this mess. He could call Laine and tell her Squirrel attacked him, but why would he be at Squirrel's in the first place?

You saw him drinking on the stoop and confronted him, chased him inside because he…because he attacked you first!

Or, Chuck could simply leave. But that wouldn't work, because of nosey ass Jenn Acton. So, he really only had one option. He found his phone at the back of the couch whose rear faced the kitchen. As he assumed, he had a miss call from the sheriff. She didn't leave a message. This was good. Now he had time to really conjure up a good story. But before he could, the words Sheriff Laine lit up the screen. The Sheriff was in parentheses.

She's going to think something's up if you don't answer. Probably, she already does.

He kicked Squirrel's shoulder. The dead man's body squelched.

"Yeah, Laine. Listen, I had an incident over at Squirrel's. You, um, need to get over here right away." Then he ended the call. After several minutes she hadn't called back, which meant she was on her way. Which meant he had to explain why his clothes were ripped to basically shreds, among other things. Laine was mostly naïve, but she was smarter than to believe Chuck would've allowed Squirrel to put up that much of a fight.

He bent over and willed the fury to come, but it never did. He flexed his muscles, thinking about how Laine had become sheriff over him, put her pretty little face at the forefront of his mind and imagined himself biting her nose off when a new thought hit him. He reached into the fridge and stole a beer, not that Squirrel would need it, and slipped out the back door.

Chapter 13

Laine didn't like the tone of Chuck's voice on the other end, insisting she meet him. How had he become so incompetent? Chuck was an independent deputy and rarely needed her guidance. Beneath the respect he showed her, she knew he thought he should be the sheriff. He had grown up in this town his entire life. She wasn't sure if the genesis of his jealousy was gender based either. Laine was the first female sheriff in Rockbridge, and she would often dismiss his ideas.

"The strong arm of the law shouldn't be bent," he would say, but part of what made her a good sheriff was her empathy. They were there to serve the community, not bring down an iron fist on folks who were only trying to get by. Rockbridge had been rocked with hard economic times. And once upon a time, Rockbridge's community looked out for one another, including the police force, which was why Laine had always wondered about Chuck's persisting in undercutting every person who broke the law. Aside from issuing a few moving violations, warnings, and bar room brawl lockups, the job didn't constitute harsh enforcing.

But someone needed to talk to Grant Hargrove. She couldn't be in two places at once. Chuck had already missed the hoof prints though. And if he needed her at Squirrel's, then whatever Chuck needed her for could prove more dire.

She pulled over with her cruiser facing Squirrel's house and called Dominique.

"Hey, need you to go the Hargrove's and question Grant," she said. "Caleb was there last night. He closed the market due to being out of power, but I was there and saw the deli counter on. Something happened at Squirrel's. Chuck needs me there.

"No, the generator wasn't running. The store has power." She swallowed hard. "Yes, tell them what happened, but only that he's, you know…no details."

She ended the call and stared intently at the A-Frame house, noticing a section of the roof sunk in. Maybe she didn't notice it earlier. Feeling for her gun, she checked the magazine and stepped out into the drizzling rain.

The streets were empty as they were these days. She walked up to the front door and knocked. After a moment, she tried the knob, but it was locked. Brow furrowed, her eyes shifted to the side.

From next door Jenn Acton peeked her head out from her front door. "I was already over there. Chuck secured the place."

Laine slowly turned her head, wearing a scowl on her face. "Okay, thanks. Go back inside now."

"What's going on?"

"Just a streak of bad luck, I suppose. We'll get it figured out."

She stared intently at Jenn, scowl never wavering, until she disappeared. Then she walked around the house and approached the back door, which hadn't seen paint in over ten years. The window in the rotting frame rattled when she knocked, yet, the door went ajar when she tried the metal knob, throwing a slice of gray light onto the kitchen linoleum.

Laine drew her gun at the familiar stench assaulting her and scrunched her nose, all without announcing herself. The computer monitor on the dining room table was off, as were all the lights. Dread hung in the atmosphere like a blanket of nightmares. She didn't need a light to see the body laying on the floor though, and that it belonged to Squirrel. Guilt stabbed her heart. She somehow felt responsible for the man's death. Afterall, she had ordered him to stay put, which proved to be a cataclysmic failure on her part. She should've let him run wild and free, like he always had, allowing the man to be who he was.

Some people can't be saved, her sister's voice, flooding her mind again. With her left hand supporting the butt of the gun, she aimed her weapon to the right and cleared the utility room, fighting off the overwhelming shock trying to take hold.

The smell was worse there. The stench rising from Squirrel's body didn't hit her until after she looked in the bathroom. Somehow his insides didn't smell nearly as strong as the primal odor.

A quick glance at the windows told her there were no signs of forced entry. After ensuring the bottom floor was clear, she clicked on her flashlight and held the beam up the stairs, listening for movement. The silence infiltrated her senses. It was too quiet to even think. She took each step one at a time, keeping the gun aimed at the open area up the stairwell. To her discouragement, the loft was empty, but the gun safe was open.

She flashed the light around the corners of the room having no need to check a closet or bathroom; Squirrel had a portable closet up here, completely unzipped, and his house only had one bathroom.

Descending the staircase, she noticed blood splatter and holes in the wood paneling, just below the landing. A shotgun lay at the front door. She missed all of it before. What else had she not noticed? Was she becoming complacent like her deputy too?

Don't fool yourself, you already were.

She drowned the thought, aimed her flashlight at the ceiling, and concluded the struggle. Someone had attacked Squirrel, forcing him to fire, and must have taken Chuck after he had called. That was the logical explanation. But nothing was orderly anymore.

Upon examining the front wall, she noted many holes which had punched through the laminate, clear past the drywall and insulation. There was a tuft of fur by the trim.

How could an animal break into a house?

"More importantly, what kind of animal could do this?"

Were the two deaths connected? Absolutely. But what was the motive? An animal didn't need one, of course, and the idea that Squirrel and Caleb could be connected other than both having been savagely murdered was foolish. Squirrel had been old enough to be his father.

The Buck Stops Here

Nick. She needed to call Nick, but dialed Chuck instead, keeping her attention on the case. Her call went straight to voicemail. "This is Chuck, leave a message." Leave a message, as if in doing so would get him to call her right back and explain everything. It did not dawn on her that Chuck could be involved, but after careful consideration, decided maybe he was. Chuck had been the first to discover Caleb, and now Squirrel, and now Chuck was gone.

She rushed to the backdoor and locked it, knowing locks only kept honest people out. Clicking off the flashlight, she stared at Squirrel's body for a moment, considering draping something over him but didn't want to disturb the scene. Her eyes welled at the sight of the racecar, the memory of Squirrel's smile and excitement he had shown upon wanting to gift it to his nephew. The tears ran when she saw the cracked picture of him and a young boy on the bank of a pond, proudly displaying a whopper for the camera, as she exited out the front door.

Outside, the wind blew and pierced her skin with thin darts of cold rain. She put her collar up, walked to her cruiser, and drove up to the house. For the first time in her career, Sheriff Abigail Laine stretched yellow police tape across a murder scene, but not without ensuring the tape was level and taut as she unwound it across the front door.

Chapter 14

"The boy was embarrassed," Dominique said over the phone. "First kiss gone bad. Then Caleb left, right after dark. Grant thought you wanted to talk to him because he would be in trouble for laughing at him, 'cause he knows you and Caleb were close. My guess? He thought his parents had found out he had girls over when he wasn't supposed to. That maybe Caleb had told on him. Like that's a crime. Needless to say, he feels terrible for it."

"That wasn't your intention," Laine said, staring through her windshield at Chuck's house, trying not to concentrate on the words *were close*.

"I know, but…I gotta say his folks are a pair," Dominique continued. "They yelled at him for having the girls over right there in front of me. I feel bad for the kid. What's up at Squirrel's?"

"He's dead, Dominique. Torn wide open."

Silence on the other end.

"Chuck wasn't there. I'm sitting outside his house now."

"Squirrel's?"

"Chuck's."

A moment later Dominique pulled up next to her with his phone still at his ear. He met her eyes, ended the call and got out. Laine stretched across the console and opened the passenger side door for him.

"What the hell?"

"You're telling me."

"So he called you, told you to meet him there, and then left?"

"Or he was taken."

"Must've been someone strong. Chuck's built like an iron wall."

She got out without another word. Dominique trailed her. Neither of them unholstered their guns.

"Torn wide open?" Dominique said, squinting in disbelief.

Laine pinched the bridge of her nose and bowed her head. Dominique took the hint and said nothing else.

#

The Buck Stops Here

Chuck lived in a two-story house, directly in the heart of the community. A mail truck drove by and the driver gave a friendly wave. Laine and Dominique nodded and stepped onto the porch.

"His truck's gone," Dominique said. He peered around the side of the house. "Lot out back's empty too."

"I'm not surprised." Laine knocked, then immediately entered.

Dominique flashed a surprising frown.

"Cover me," Laine said, stepping inside. "Chuck! It's me. I got Dominique here too. You home?"

Something misted in the corner of the room, startling them both. Laine's head quickly snapped in the direction of the sound.

"Automatic sprayer," she said, and instantly, the air filled with the scent of warm apple pie.

They walked through the first floor, opening every door, glancing in every corner of the open layout. A few minutes passed and they split up, Dominique taking the basement, Laine the upstairs where two bedrooms and a full bath were.

She entered the bathroom and thought maybe the mister would be better used in here. Whiskers littered the sink, atop of which lay a toothbrush with frayed bristles. Nothing behind the shower curtain. Brown streaks in the toilet.

Chuck had turned one of the bedrooms into an office, where only a laptop sat on a tiny desk. Hanging on the wall above the desk was a movie poster with Uma Thurman holding a cigarette, looking sultry. Laine touched the mousepad. The screen lit up, requesting a password. She closed it and thought twice about taking it but decided to leave it in case she was overreacting.

"Sheriff!" Dominique's voice from the basement, coming through the vents.

Before she took the stairs, Laine went into the other bedroom. Here, a chest of drawers was open. Socks, jeans, and flannels were piled haphazardly atop one another. One would have to take time to organize them neatly before the drawers could close.

Someone packed in a hurry.

Grabbing the handrail, she sped down the staircase, through the living room, and halted at the top of the basement stairs.

"Dominique!"

A beat passed before he answered. "Get down here, Sheriff. Please."

She wiped her brow and descended, her footfalls echoing below her. Dominique came into view, backing up against the adjacent concrete wall with his arm held up, face buried in his elbow. With his other arm he pointed forward.

With one hand on the handrail, Laine leaned forward and removed her flashlight, clicking it on with her thumb. Her eyes followed the beam which followed the direction in which Dominique was pointing.

There, in the dingy basement, the beam captured a million dust motes. Through the haze hung the most wretched stink of flesh and rot, something Laine imagined could only happen in the cold attic of a deranged mind.

Two hooks suspended the body of a white-tailed buck, cavity open, completely dissected. It served as a headdress for one Chuck Edwards, whose naked body wore the animal like a savage mountain hunter.

Chapter 15

Chuck pounded the beer he got from Squirrel's fridge while traveling a cool thirty-five. The fat tires on his Dodge Ram hugged the steep turns. He turned up the radio, increasing the volume of the static coming through the speakers.

His destination loomed five miles away, and it would take him all of twenty minutes to reach it. The storm had made the roads slick, and the winding cliffs didn't exactly make for prime cruising. But he choogled along, chomping on a fat wad of Levi Garret while pouring beer into the clean side of his mouth, only spitting brown juice into a Styrofoam cup on occasion.

Chuck's roots ran deep up here. His grandmother had bought Edward's Escape in the eighties and retired there. After her heart stopped, the getaway resort became his mother's, who had no use for it except for the occasional Scentsy party. Chuck practically lived there all summer long, but now that he had found what he called The Fury, he decided the cabin would make the perfect place to wait. And if he was right, Laine would eventually find his place in Rockbridge empty and come looking, with Dominique no doubt, up there. Two against one. Really, one against one. Dominique might have been a big tough guy in Columbus, busting hookers and dealers at The Hilltop, but this wasn't the city, and Chuck was no pimp or pill slinger. What he had in store for him, and her, would require a deeper understanding about ancient evils, and those few who did understand could never be prepared for what Chuck had become, which was only a shell of what he once was.

In mid-September, as the horizon above the hills glinted against the forest, Chuck Edwards had walked onto the top deck of Edward's Escape with a newspaper tucked under his arm.

He had been in an exceptionally good mood that day, but why, he could not recall. Flashes of that day skittered on the edge of a thin tether clinging to his mind. He only remembered moments of it, like right before you have a bad accident; that initial impact, slice, or thrown punch glimpsed in a series of pictographs. The mind had a devious way of saving oneself from such horrible recollections, protecting it as if the threat still remained. And in Chuck's case, what had not only terrorized him had also became a *part* of him, lingering on well after initial incubation.

The Buck Stops Here

He had solved the crossword puzzle remarkably fast, but it was too early for a flick yet, and he wanted to listen to the cicadas whirl a little while longer, to the occasional meadowlark sing, to the breeze whispering through fat leaves.

Earlier, he had checked the levels of the hot tub. Now, he flicked the jets on and brought the water inside to a rolling boil. His feet ached something fierce from having jogged two and a half miles that morning, a new personal best. A twenty-ounce ribeye lay marinating in the fridge for him to grill after his soak.

Yes, a good day indeed for any bachelor who had already settled down comfortably without marriage or children. If they could look at him now, they wouldn't think of him as the lanky poor boy whose walk caused his classmates to guffaw when he walked down the hallway, whose brace-covered bucked teeth had made them motion their hands like they were brushing two massive pieces of stone jutting from their front lip, whose most awkward moment came when a freshman had bushed him his senior year. Ah yes, if they could look at him now, living the good life.

Women didn't take to Chuck as well as he took to them. Neither did men. He tried in the academy and that went south real fast. He had become close to one Eddie Fringe. They were boys, as the lingo went, and after loading up at The Station in Athens, went back to Eddie's for a nightcap. Eddie had stared into his eyes a moment too long. Apparently, Eddie just had too much Jager because before he knew it, Chuck had planted one on him without even really wanting to. He just wanted to know what kissing another man felt like. Eddie had returned the gesture by planting his fist onto Chuck's left eye. The next day, Eddie wasn't in class. He had promptly disenrolled himself from the academy.

Chuck had a profile on all the typical dating apps but found out fast he was not the only one who lied on their profile. Mainly, his dates stretched the truth about their occupation, some their build, but mostly in his experience, it was their jobs they were ashamed of. Dating went on that way for a while for Chuck, until the notifications no longer gave him the endorphin rush he once craved.

He stood in the center of the breeze, letting the wind kiss his cheeks, ears, and hair. He had regretted turning on the hot tub before he walked down the two-story staircase. Down here, the grass was soft. No worries. Let it run. So he walked into the woods, hoping to listen to nature breathe a little while longer.

A sizable stick lay near. He picked it up, stabbed it into the dirt, and hiked the trail leading to an overlook of a waterfall. This waterfall had caused a few deaths ever since he had helped build a wooden barricade across the edge, yet somehow people (mostly out-of-towners trying to impress their significant other) managed to fall to their demise on the rocky bottom below it. For no particular reason, he decided he wanted to know what it felt like to be up there. His intention wasn't to impress anyone. He was alone after all. He simply wanted to feel the sensation of being above everything, curious if he were to accidentally slip, would the sudden rush of wanting to live grip him.

But Chuck never made it to the top of the waterfall. Instead, he approached the pool in which the fountain fed, watching frothy water undulate, wondering what could be down there. Would there be earrings, necklaces, yellow bones and teeth? Treasure? He was pretty sure someone had left goggles somewhere in the storage bin on the deck. But that eddy, sucking up twigs and tall grass underneath the cascading water, kept him there.

Dipping the end of his walking stick into the water, his gaze followed the path of the eddy. He stared, swirling the stick around and around, making a tiny whirlpool of his own when something behind him cackled.

He turned and saw a buck, the biggest deer he had ever seen. 16-points donned its antlered head. Its hind quarters swelled in sunlight seeping through the trees. Despite its magnificence, deer didn't cackle, so this one must have stepped on a branch or a blanket of foliage—it was hard to tell as the deer stood in the shadows of the woods—but it definitely hadn't laughed out loud. No way.

He watched the buck for a moment, slack jawed from its huge eyes and stoic stance. Chuck marveled, thinking the deer's image would look fine in a golden frame, chiseled body and all, when its ears pricked up at something Chuck didn't or couldn't hear. Then it pranced away in four quick dashes.

Chuck wished he had brought his phone to snap its picture, but Sheriff Laine was notorious for calling him on his day off, wanting him to cover for her for one thing or another. Usually, it had to do with useless Nick or his bratty-ass kid Caleb. They deserved each other, those three, and she had no business being a sheriff because of it. The two of them constantly pulled her away from her duties, made her softer as a law enforcer, and were so apparently wonderful that she felt the need to tell Chuck about how wonderful they were every chance she got.

Heart still thumping, Chuck returned his gaze to the water, feeling a little sorry for himself. He had lobbied harder than Laine for sheriff, going door to door, setting up community drives, and letting people off with a warning whenever they rolled through a stop sign. But most of those people had been out-of-towners, only coming and going for the busy summer months to cozy up in a cabin or float down the Hocking Livery. Still, he thought maybe word would get around that Deputy Edwards was a fine man and one you could trust, even with the locals. Especially with the locals. However, the locals had spoken up. The majority voted for Abigail Laine. She got the title, pay increase, and all the accolades.

Even though he had Edward's Escape, his elation continued slipping away. He tossed the stick into the pool. And while trying to force the mope out of himself while turning toward the direction he had come, something clamped down on his shoulder.

He had smelled something awful, but thought it was just a dead animal rotting away nearby. When he completed the turn, he found the source of the odor standing at chest height.

"My god." Chuck reeled back, felt the ground give under him, and reached an arm out. His foot lost purchase, and he smacked the ground hard. He lay there for a moment, blinking at the two hooves in front of him, waiting for them to kick at him, waiting for the jolt of the impact to dissipate. The hooves only stood there amongst leaves curling at the edges.

Deer were shy. They didn't hunt.

Pain blossomed in his chest. His fright turned to rage. If he had to slap a deer, he would. He hoisted himself up, wiping debris and sweat from his face. Standing full bore, toe to toe, was the buck he had seen just a moment ago. Something wiggled about its face though, across the slant of its brown furry nose, and disappeared into both pupils.

The buck scraped a front hoof against the ground, as if to charge, then shook its head, as if reconsidering. Chuck dipped to the left, barely escaping the sharpened rack assaulting the space between them.

The Buck Stops Here

Small patters fell nearby, the sound of rain, but this came from under the deer. Chuck thought maybe the animal was defecating until he realized pieces of flesh began falling from its body.

He took a step back, thinking the smell came from the deer, which had to be in clear discomfort because long parasites writhed within the deer's exposed ribcage. Within the parasite's translucent body glowed red veins, the same color as the deer's eyes. Funny. He hadn't noticed them change color.

Chuck had seen a movie once where some friends went to a cabin and came across a similar situation. In that film, the military was already ahead of the curve. Soon, he thought, the sound of choppers would come from above. Then he would race out of the woods and wave them down. They would need him. He had lived here his entire life.

Instead of a Hollywood rescue, the deer lurched forward and vomited. A stringy rope of something hung from its mouth then quickly disappeared back up the throat.

Chuck ran, ignoring the briar patches and fallen branches, which made up the entire path, until a quarter mile of woods separated him from the falls. Panting, he bent over and placed his hands upon his knees before daring a look over his shoulder. Only the forest stared back.

The wound on his shoulder announced itself by sending sharp sensations down his back and legs. He hobbled up to the cabin, through the patio doors below the deck, and heaved himself against the dining room table. Pain stricken, he couldn't move at first, then thought, *I got a form of mad cow disease!* Only this disease didn't wait to infiltrate his flesh. Sucking noises soon invaded his ear. He fought through the cramps, but only managed to fall to the hardwood floor. He shoved a trembling hand across his body, yet it only moved an inch at a time. Biting at his collar, his shirt, anything to achieve a grip on his flannel, his fingers suddenly wiggled. No longer in an arthritic pose, the fingers grasped the buttons and popped them open one a time.

His teeth grinded together as he unpeeled the fabric from his skin. Several marks bled atop his shoulder, and within those marks swam a translucent parasite, pulsing in red.

His thumb and forefinger met, closing in on the intruder. If only he had his utility knife, he could dig it out, but the worm seemed content at the surface where black lines bolted forth like hell lightning.

If I can just get my fingers onto it...

The wipers shook him from the memory. Sweat beaded across his forehead and went unnoticed. He nearly veered off the road from the recollection which vanished from his memory the moment it began.

"Ah, shit!" He righted the truck, wiped his brow, and sped up a curve. Where had that memory come from? He hadn't thought of it in so long. In the beginning when he had first contracted the fury, he knew he had killed. Small animals at first: squirrels, birds, the occasional fox, but had moved up the food chain and graduated to people. He didn't remember ever attacking anyone. He only knew traces of their scent brought the image of wide, terrified eyes into his mind. However, the last few, the ones most deserving, had been stored somewhere in his head. Chuck assumed the parasite had grown like a long vein connecting to all his necessary parts to transform him into a supreme warrior. Combined with his ambition, Chuck felt he was nearly invincible to any threat the town could pose. The best part for him? He was finally doing something about them.

Tires ate up gravel, clinking against the pick-up's undercarriage. Edward's Escape awaited him, along with the fury.

Chapter 16

"How…" Dominique said, unblinking.

"His body is decomposing," Laine said. "It can't be. He just called me. This couldn't have happened"—her head shook—"that quick."

She stared at the head dress for so long Dominique didn't wait for her to excuse him. The sound of his footsteps soon flooded the basement. Several minutes passed before Laine even realized he had left her down there alone.

"Some kind of ritual? A rite maybe?" She turned to Dominique, but she only saw the gray brick wall.

"Up here, Sheriff."

He must have been watching her. Before she climbed the stairs, she snapped a photo of the scene. She did not see anything else in the small basement. She could've dug through the crawl space down there but wasn't going any further without reinforcements. The matter had changed from a small-town murder to a deep dive into psychological terror.

Heavy feet carried her up the steps.

When she reached Dominique she vomited much like Nick had that morning. Wiping her mouth clean, she took a deep breath. "It's like someone unzipped him and everything came falling out."

Dominique's bottom lip quivered. "No person could do this to someone, not without careful consideration. I mean, this isn't an impromptu murder we're dealing with. Someone planned this."

"Yeah, I know, I just gotta—" she wretched again, fighting off the urge to crawl into a ball and wish this day away. "Hooo, oh boy. Okay. Let's go back to the station and make some calls. We need help, Dominique."

"Help? Damn. We need the FBI!"

"Have you been keeping up with Michael's blog?"

"Nah. I went home and took a nap after you dismissed me. Tried to at least."

Well, I managed to, she thought. *Guess that makes me terrible.* But she knew Dominique didn't mean it in that way. He didn't even know she had napped, but the guilt for having done so remained.

"Okay, let's get the hell outta here. Put up the tape, will ya?"

She left without waiting for him to answer.

The Buck Stops Here

After getting into the cruiser and waiting for Dominque to finish closing off the house, she called Steven, hoping he could give her information regarding Caleb's death.

"I can tell ya it was sharp and it wasn't clean," Steven said. "My guess? The end of a wide hatchet is what did it."

Of course, hatchets did not hover around slicing the heads off teenage boys. The nearest hardware store consisted of a Walmart in Athens county and good luck trying to get surveillance on that.

"Ain't had the body but for a few hours," he said. "Some guy got drunk and went off the road in Nelsonville, wrapped himself around a guardrail. He was riding a motorcycle. He beat Caleb here."

"Call me if you find anything," she said, not appreciating Steven's humorous tone, and hung up.

Dominique avoided eye contact with her as he got into his cruiser. He trailed her through town, and soon stopped in the middle of the road where a mob awaited outside the The Hill, the local dive.

Chapter 17

The rain had finally stopped, and Laine recognized everyone. From Michael, the town's beat reporter, to Jenn Acton, recording the scene on her ridiculously large phone, all the way to Big Bad Bill. He had swapped his rainslicker for a leather jacket which had a skull and crossbones on the back. A camouflaged container was strapped to Corey Kessler; she could now see it since he had turned and faced the mob, holding a long metal rod in his hand. Various weapons, mostly rifles, lifted to the sky.

Laine let it be known they'd better move by hitting the flashers. But the mob stayed, unwilling to let her pass despite her honking the horn and bathing them in red and blue.

Her chin jutted as she threw the cruiser in park. Cold droplets of rain pooling on her jacket collar splashed onto her neck. She didn't even flinch.

"What's this all about, Bill?" she said as she got out, hearing Dominique's door slam behind her.

"We's fixin' to fight the monsters invading this town, that's what!"

A collective "yeah!" followed.

"Just get back inside and we'll talk about what's going on," Dominique said, joining Laine in the stand-off.

"He's right," Laine said, although she wasn't thrilled with the idea of herding angry folks armed to the gills into a bar.

A baseball bat slipped from Michael's shoulder and landed in the palm of his hand. "Then what? You gonna tell us all to go home and let you take care of it? Just like you took care of Caleb? And where's Squirrel? Saw the police tape up at his house on the way over here. We sooner assume you're keeping information, like they do in Roswell, than be honest with us."

"For Christ's sake, Michael, get inside!" She pointed stoically at The Hill and knew once she got him inside the rest would follow. He was as boisterous as they came, and also claimed to be a descendent of renowned Civil War general William T. Sherman. Whether or not the latter was true was up for debate, but everyone believed it, including Bill, who fired a shot into the air.

Dominique went to draw his gun, but Laine grabbed his wrist.

"You heard her," Bill said. "Inside!"

Grumbling followed, and the crowd clambered into the bar.

The Buck Stops Here

"They're brave in ignorance," Dominique said. "Anyone of them had seen what we had, and they'd be hiding behind locked doors."

Laine flung out her arms, brushing rainwater from her sleeve as she entered The Hill. Dominique followed, allowing the screen door rattle against the jamb behind him. Those who were not on barstools stood in the corner, over by the bathroom. The mob surrounded Laine and her officer in an almost perfect horseshoe. Despite the dim lighting, Laine knew all the faces, many of whom, if not all, were responsible for the title Sheriff printed across the back of her jacket.

After scanning her people she was paid to protect, she decided the only way to discourage them was to be as blunt as possible. She cleared her throat. Her chest rose.

"Caleb Welsh is dead. He was decapitated." She suspected they knew this already because no one even groaned.

"Hobbes Oliver, who we all know as Squirrel, is also dead. He was first rammed into his living room wall before his chest was ripped open."

Some stirred at this, while others broke eye contact with her.

"Chuck Edwards is also dead."

A collective sigh followed this bit of news. Now that she had their attention and was in control, even in this moment, she continued, scolding them as if being punished.

"His body is in his basement right now, practically mummified, wearing the body of a deer like it was a bathrobe. Now, do you mind telling me and Dominique where exactly you all were planning on going?" She swallowed hard, amazed at how easily the words came out, more amazed at the relief she felt for saying them.

"We were going to search the town, Sheriff, the one thing you didn't do, the one thing you should've done," Michael said.

He approached her from the left, camera hanging around his neck. His handmade Press tag jutting from the band of his fedora. She noticed several more index cards in the breast pocket of his faded black oxford shirt, fresh cards to replace the ones that fell out, she guessed. His mustache looked as if it had been stenciled on. She always wanted to take a large pink rubber eraser to it. "So, the question begs, why didn't you?"

"We did and found a hoof print and a ball of fur with a long human hair entangled in it. But hair analysis is proven to be unreliable anyway because scientists do not have population-based databases. They cannot compare samples so they can't determine their characteristics. All we are left with are the prints and the murders. How about you keep the speculating to us, Michael, and worry about not creating a frenzy with your blog, which I haven't had the pleasure of reading today."

"Ha! A hoof print!" Michael splayed his hands apart. "A hoof print. Sure it wasn't a print the size of my shin? My god, everybody, we got Bigfoot on our hands!"

No one laughed. Michael's face flushed red, but before he went slithering back into the crowd he added, "We should've made Chuck sheriff. At least he'd still be alive."

Folks looked at each other, nodding along with the man's words.

"We were fools to believe you could protect this town!" Michael pointed at her, and Big Bad Bill hollered, "He's right! It's your fault our taxes was raised!"

The words didn't sting, Laine had checked her ego the moment she became sheriff, if she ever had one to begin with, and decided even Sherlock Holmes would have a difficult time trying to solve the heinous murders occurring in the sleepy town of Rockbridge. Although, she started to wish she would have handled her delivery with a little dignity and grace.

"Bill, you don't even know what you're talking about," Dominique said. "This matter is over our heads. Three people have been brutally murdered within nine hours of each other. For all we know—"

The killer is among us, Abigail thought, but she didn't need them turning against each other.

"The killer is out there," she said instead, finishing Dominique's sentence, "which is why you all need to go home and look out for each other."

"I say," Michael said, "killer should be plural, as in killers, and you need our help in finding them."

A sharp whistle cut the air and Cory and Bill parted way, among several others, to the source. Sitting on a bar stool with her back to Laine and Dominique sat Miss Adley. She spun around with her head low, wearing a camo ballcap. She looked ten years younger to Laine when she lifted her head, face glowing with a mystic aura.

"I assume you didn't read my statement," she said to Laine.

"Haven't had the time." Laine's impatience grew, feeling precious seconds ticking away, but this fire needed put out first.

"You wanna get this thing? You gotta hit it where it counts." She patted the right side of her chest.

"In the boob?" Bill said.

Adley glared at him, then shifted her gaze back to Laine. "In the heart. It's where it incubates and grows until there's nothing left to consume, which is why you saw Chuck Edwards's body in his basement. That's the real Chuck Edwards. The one who's been walking around this town the last few weeks…hasn't been Chuck at all."

Michael smirked while everyone else went slack jawed.

"The mother's heart beats behind the falls. You all think I'm crazy because I report having seen and heard things that can't be explained back in the woods behind my home. But this? It dates back hundreds of years, before Rockbridge was settled. It's been here the entire time."

"Why wait 'til now to come out then?" Michael said, holding a notepad but not actually writing anything down.

"Its food source is ripe. Tell me, when was the last time any of you visited one another when you didn't need something? We're so consumed with ourselves, we've completely forgotten how to take care of our community. And now it's here, ready to wipe us out, until there's nothing left but bulldozers and backhoes paving way for a new community full of condominiums, coffee shops, and restaurants. Plenty of activity. At least, enough to convince it a source of togetherness exists.

"It feeds on our jealousy. Too busy keepin' up with the Joneses instead of focusing your concerns on your neighbor. Sure, the economy is great. We had a prosperous summer. I see you driving around in your four-door trucks, white glove service walking big tv's into our homes. Whatever happened to the block parties? We used to have four a year. Hell, even Maggie's felt the hit."

Adley turned to Maggie Parks who stood behind the bar, the only woman in Rockbridge who could pull off pigtails and glasses at thirty without trying to look virtuous. She simply looked away as Adley continued.

"Dart league, euchre nights. Nonexistent."

Rubbing his thin mustache, Michael said, "and what makes you the expert on this, Adley?"

The Buck Stops Here

Everyone's head turned from Steven to Miss Adley. "My grandparents were the last ones to be infected. They turned on each other, sparring at the covered bridge you and Bill used to catch minnows under."

Bill and Michael's eyes shifted to the side before lowering.

"Did you think I forgot? You two were inseparable. Now you're at each other's throats over who's responsible for that damn tree and its brittle branches. For the record, it's on the property line. You're both at fault."

Adley then took a nip of brown liquid from a glass.

"I was staying with my grandparents when it happened. Smelled something awful leaking underneath the door, then I heard a crash, and a noise I can only describe as an animal in pain. When I left the bedroom, the front door was wide open. I thought someone broke in, so I went back inside and crawled through my bedroom window. Phones weren't portable back then. They had only one and theirs was in the kitchen, you see.

"Outside, the crickets chirped, and in a flash, I saw one deer chasing another, only they both ran on their hind legs. I ran in the opposite direction, toward Doug Crenshaw's house. He was the sheriff back then. From the dale overlooking the town, I had a clear view of the bridge underneath a three-quarter moon."

"I thought werewolves only transformed during a full moon," Corey said.

"These ain't werewolves," Adley said, picking up a crossbow no one noticed leaning against the bar and slamming the stock against the floor. "Now let me finish. The racks were huge, tangling within one another." Adley closed her eyes, barely unable to finish, and drew a deep breath. "Then both deer fell. I dared a looksee by moving further along the dale and there were Gramma Emma and Granpa Hoit, laying next to each other. Part of them," she held up her hand here, "part of them was still animal."

"Where was their real bodies then?" Michael said.

"Those were their real bodies. What Charles did, rather, what the parasite did, was play to a new host."

"Couldn't we just, I don't know, burn Charles's real body then and put an end to all this?" Dominique said.

"When the parasite resurrects itself, it makes a sacrifice. Chuck Edwards sacrificed his body, unwillingly I'm sure, and became the supreme host."

"Who was the supreme host when you were a little girl," Laine said, "when all this happened?"

"Never did find it. If Crenshaw did, he didn't share that information with me."

"We gotta find Crenshaw!" someone in the back said.

"Can't," Adley said. "He's been dead and gone since the nineties."

"Oh, man!" Big Bad Bill said. "You expect us to believe that?"

"No, I don't. But I do expect you to come along. They're right, sheriff. We do need their help, and I got a plan."

Chapter 18

The air was quiet except for fine droplets of rain dripping from the eaves of a once familiar place. Beyond towering oak pillars were many windows with diamond-shaped grids, jutting gables, and a porch stretching the entire length of the perplexing structure. These qualities pulsed in hues of red and green. All still in dichromacy vision.

The beast lurched forward. Human hands splayed upon moist brick until the true form pierced the vessel of flesh the parasite had overtaken. This body was decomposing. A strip of skin here, an ear there. Random tufts of hair fell until jutting tusks protruded around the skull. Coarse brown fur sprouted along the face, elongated from the parasite's rage. Sneakers split, making room for hooves the size of anvils.

New muscle, chiseled and lean, bulged through the soft fabric entrapping the vessel. Two more hooves, gleaming with a razor's edge, came forth from underneath the wrists. A snapping of the jaw became the genesis of a newly formed head, ripe with red glowing eyes and blunt teeth.

The final part of him desperately holding on had let go. The parasite had taken full control of its host.

When it rose, the primeval mutation once known as Chuck Edwards first saw the head of a lion clutching a brass ring in its maw festooned to the front door of the elaborate construct. The beast raised its chin at the predator, waiting for it to make the first move. Organically, an urge to flee flooded its instincts. Primally though, it was primed to rage.

From the belly of the beast rose an anger unparallel to what any human had ever felt. A quick slash cleaved the lion head in two, followed by a satisfying clank when it landed. The beast sent its hoof into the better half still bolted to the door, creating a deep groove where the knocker once hung.

The easy kill did not satisfy. There was neither agony nor remorse from the prey. The lion lay there, angry eyes glaring up at the beast. This one had already been dead, it seemed.

The beast raised its head and stared beyond the forest.

Slaughter lay at the forefront of its needs and this place, wherever it was, did not meet the criteria for such activity. Twenty miles away was where the beast would dance, smack dab in the ever-loving place of rot it had come to be.

Chapter 19

I'm just going to do it now, Nick thought. *I'm gonna tip this chair over and give myself what I deserve.*

All the anger had left Nick Welsh. Now that his home looked as if a tornado had torn through it, depression wracked him. The thought of not only losing a child but being the one responsible for their death shouted at him, reprimanding him for his imprudence. He thought maybe he was only dreaming when he found himself awake, naked and confused, running around trees, trying to find his way home that morning.

The first time the spell had gripped him, he was positive senility had caused his lack of memory and behavior. Maybe he had inherited the disease from his grandfather after all. But it had only happened just the one time, until a few weeks ago. And this morning. But that rationale confused him. He was only forty-five.

Nick was baffled about why he was out there in the first place and, to make matters worse, his bowels went south uncontrollably when he got home. And as he sat on the toilet, flushing out the swimming sensation in his stomach, flashes of him running amok began striking his mind. Within these glimpses, Nick had incredible speed and power. His senses were heightened. He could actually smell the animals around him and hear them pattering to and fro, as if teasing him, daring him into a chase.

Fourteen days ago, when Nick first blacked out, he found a dog at his feet when he awoke. The dog was mangy and had a terrible scar below one eye. It had to be feral. He practically knew every dog in town, none of which had the characteristics of neglect, let alone of a wolf. Nick's left foot had grazed it. He still remembered the warm, wet sensation it left.

He couldn't help but think how things would have been different had he never got divorced or how Caleb would still be alive if he had married Abigail after. Perhaps then he would not have been taking a stroll in the woods in the first place.

Marriage, ha! How'd that thought get in here? He thought only the worst of sins were allowed inside when one had an extension cord around their neck. Speaking of, he tried tucking his fingers underneath the cord, but it was too damn tight. On purpose. How could he forget? Instead of wicking away the sweat tickling his skin, Nick only managed to aggravate the chafing underneath his Adam's apple.

Better do it now before I chicken out. He wanted Caleb at the front and center of his thoughts before darkness met him. His son at least deserved that. And in a way Nick supposed he did too. He couldn't be sure he was the one who had murdered Caleb, but what else could've beheaded his only child? For one, the source of his blackouts could have been responsible. The deer that had bit him several weeks ago had looked a little maniacal, as if it had frolicked in a pool of toxic waste. Rabies explained that, he guessed. And so far, he hadn't contracted the disease. And because he went out into the woods so often, Nick had gotten tested after the bite, which had healed without complications rather quickly. Within three days there wasn't so much as a scar on his wrist where the deer had bit him before frightenedly running away. With no other reason to foster a source, he had to be the killer.

His weight shifted back to front as he held onto the cord tied around an exposed rafter in the ceiling. Plaster crumbled and sprinkled onto his shoulders. In fact, he was covered with the stuff from using a Sawzall to cut the hole in the first place, ensuring a satisfying death. The last thing he wanted was to tie the cord to a fixture, only to have it give under his weight.

The chair whined against the wood flooring. Nick blew up an image of Caleb in his mind. Looking sad, the image of the boy slowly blinked as if anticipating his father to join him in the afterlife. God, Nick dreaded an afterlife. In the event his soul would perish in the great beyond, rather than shutting off like a satisfying click of a light, he would have to carry the burden of Caleb's death with him.

A truck passed his bay window outside, and then another. Soon, a convoy appeared on Nick's road consisting mostly of pickup trucks, many of which he recognized. Had someone caught wind of his suicide? Had the entire town come to save him?

The vehicles were in a hurry and had come in droves. At least a dozen passed before he saw Abigail's cruiser turning into his driveway.

He wouldn't allow her to find him dead and certainly not in the middle of hanging himself. She had a key and his car was parked outside even though he was supposed to be on the road to see Faith, his ex-wife.

He had told her about Caleb, said he was packing to come see her.

"I don't need you right now, Nick. Who I need is Caleb!" was what she had said before she abruptly hung up, and those words stung because so did he.

Abigail was busy trying to find the killer and Nick didn't want to interfere with the case, knowing her consoling him would only take away from it. With no one to turn to, he figured he would make life easier for everyone.

But what if his suicide somehow led Abigail to believe that he was responsible? What if she found his torn clothes from this morning buried deep in his garbage? The dead couldn't speak for themselves. Caleb would've died in vain, his daddy a murderous tramp, trying to cover up, well, what exactly?

Nick placed all his weight on the chair and steadied the legs. A butcher knife lay on the oven from earlier when he learned he could not stomach slashing his own throat. He reached for the knife now, uncaring if he nicked his neck again while trying to get the cord free. A small price compared to the bigger purchase he was flirting with.

The toe of his sneaker grazed the knife's wooden handle, too wide for him to even grip with two fingers, yet he tried anyway, attempting to knock the knife into the air, grasp it with both feet while holding onto the cord, and bringing his feet up so he could snag it with the other hand. This maneuver would take an extreme amount of core strength he knew he didn't have, but it was his only chance.

Kicking at the air, he managed to move the handle so that a section of it managed to hang over the oven. He wasn't sure if the oven's raised edge would prevent the knife from somersaulting toward him, so he climbed upon the dining room table, which made breathing a whole hell of a lot easier.

Sweat ran down his face and pooled around his neck. Heart pounding, he now felt a little embarrassed and pitied himself the more he watched the knife. Laine must be wondering what he was doing standing on the table. Then, as if a light bulb had flashed above his head, he began working the knot out of the cord with both hands. He had given himself an easy out without even realizing it. With the chair only feet away, he scooted it below the dangling cord after freeing himself. Rubbing his neck, he climbed upon the chair. With the knife in his other hand, he sliced the cord free.

He wouldn't be able to explain the damage to his home. At least not yet, but he would live long enough to come up with a good story if the time came.

Chapter 20

Everyone piled into their vehicles, including Adley, who was the first to pull out from The Hill's parking lot. Laine thought the mission was insane: the town follows little old Miss Adley up to Hocking Hills to kill a were-deer.

But here they were, doing exactly that.

"Corey," Laine said, before getting into her cruiser, calling to him over several pick-ups. "Is that a flamethrower?"

Corey only smiled.

"Where did you get a flamethrower?"

"Amazon, what you think?"

"You're bringing a flamethrower to the woods? Huh-uh. Put it away and never use it. Ever."

"Damn!" Corey shimmied the tank off his back and placed it in someone's truck bed.

"I'm serious!"

"Yeah, yeah, I heard ya." He lit a smoke and got into Big Bad Bill's company truck that had B3 Plumbing boldly etched on both sides of the doors. Everybody knew what the three B's stood for.

They talked it over and thought it best if everyone rode with someone, to avoid cramping the road and their destination. It wasn't lost on her what else waited at Edward's Escape besides an alleged nest of evil.

Dominique rode with her. He rubbed his face, dug his palms into his eyes. "I can't believe we're doing this."

"Me either, but you heard Adley. I mean, it does make sense."

"Strangely, yes, it does."

She glanced at her deputy. "Look, we take the fifteen minute drive up there to find her phantom. The place will be empty. Maybe. Maybe not. If it is, we drive back and continue the investigation." She vehemently shook her head. "But, I dunno, everything we have seen so far, it all adds up."

"I don't believe in magic, good or bad." A few seconds passed and Dominique looked at her in astonishment after she didn't respond with, "I don't either".

That's because Laine thought there was magic all around, always had been. There were too many things in this world unexplained. Believers were often labeled as either conspiracists or people of God, claiming to have witnessed miracles. Others were dismissed, like Miss Adley had been. All things unexplained pointed in the direction of the loonies, the ill-minded, ones whose brains were perhaps chemically imbalanced if not radicalized by dark web theories or cultists. And even though the theory of an ancient parasite living behind Edward's Escape did not exactly fit into any of those categories, perhaps science could explain how such an organism could infect a human. She recalled a designer drug called Flakka, or bath salts, which could cause someone to eat the flesh off someone else. If a zombie drug existed, then why couldn't a were-infection? All of this of course, unless you were a person of God, in which case, the rapture would be another perfectly acceptable explanation.

Everyone was bumper to bumper. In her peripheral she noticed Dominique still looking at her after stating his disbelief in magic.

"Maybe if you hit the lights, got up front, this would move things along," he said.

His suggestion snapped her from thought. "Good idea. I'll wait until we get out of town." But she noticed Nick's vehicle in the driveway. Curious why he hadn't left to see Faith, she pulled in.

"What are we doing here?" Dominique said.

Practically mumbling, she said, "He was supposed to visit his ex-wife."

"Oh." Dominque's impatient thumbs beat on his leg. He noticed a notebook on Laine's dash. CONFIDENTIAL was written diagonally across the cover in black marker.

"May I?" he said, reaching for the notebook.

"Sure." She stared at the house for a moment, then pulled away and decided to call Nick instead.

Chapter 21

Nick watched Laine's cruiser pull out and felt guilty for allowing her to leave. "No secrets between us," they had promised each other one evening after binging Season One of *You* on Netflix. Here Nick stood holding the frayed end of an extension cord in his hand, withholding the biggest secret of his life.

He had the power to transform himself into a monstrous predator. What exactly, he wasn't sure, only that as of late, glimpses of his nightly outings had haunted him randomly throughout the day. Something wasn't right, something his doctor didn't have the resources to detect when he got the rabies shot.

He shuffled backward until the back of his legs touched the seat of the chair. He plopped down and put his face in his hands, ran them through his greasy hair while the cord fell lazily from his grasp when a thought hit him.

What if the town had found the real killer and were on their way to burn them at the stake? Better yet, stone them! Why else would Abigail be amid a convoy full of their neighbors?

A wry smile crept across Nick's face. Something deep within him began to burn. He had never felt so alive. Out of all the irrational events in the last twenty-four hours there was still time left for daft action.

What to bring, he thought while wriggling his fingers.

He scanned the kitchen before hurrying into the living room. A fire poker leaned against the fireplace. The Sawzall lay in the corner by the hallway. A finger trembling with excitement met his chin. Other than the butcher knife, he could not recall having owned a serious weapon. He never had the need while living in Rockbridge.

The garage!

He ran back through the kitchen. Hedge shears, a weed whacker, and a shovel all lined the well-organized pegboard on one wall inside the garage. He pulled a string and the garage flooded with light from the naked bulb above him. A shimmer caught his gauge. Slowly turning, following the gleam, hung a chainsaw.

Quickly he ran to it, hefting it from the hook, and brandished the blade. The satisfying splash of gasoline filled one ear. He hit the garage door opener, chainsaw at his side. But his triumphant exit was cut short because he needed to go back inside and get his car keys. The exhilaration left him. The house was a mess. They could've been anywhere.

And the convoy was over.

The Buck Stops Here

As he headed back inside, an offending stink struck him. His stomach began squirming and that squirming leeched tentacles inside him, writhing through his veins and arteries. Left eye twitching, a doomed panic slammed him square in the chest. He poised the chainsaw, keeping the starter between his thumb and forefinger. Nick didn't know how or why but he felt a presence lurking near. Something sinister. Otherworldly.

His eyes dilated. He felt his irises shift. The black sheen on the road, the hunter green quality of his Chrysler, even the sky, gray and ominous, had a tint to it he couldn't quite describe.

The top button on his flannel popped and rolled like a tire over the concrete floor until it fell hopelessly on its side somewhere along the driveway. The next button did the same.

Nick wrenched over as sharp pangs shot through his back, up his neck, and around his temples. The chainsaw rattled against the floor and he nearly placed his palms atop the blade when he dropped to his knees. The feeling of digesting an entire loaf of bread nestled in his stomach.

The virus is back. I'm gonna blow my pants out!

His pants definitely tore apart, but not due to a blast from his colon. His knees had buckled inward to allow space for animalistic quarters while his head felt like something was being pried from his skull. It was as if he had six talons hidden on either side of his head and they had finally decided to come out. Through all the tearing and ripping of both flesh and cloth, Nick Welsh heard heavy breathing.

When Faith had served him the divorce papers, the memory of the sound the manilla file made when he tore it in two came to him as the pain continued. His fingers and knuckles curled past his wrists. He imagined his toes had done the same because he no longer felt unsteady there on the garage floor. His vision blurred as if someone had hit a fast-forward button, only, his surroundings occurred in real time. Brittle bone cracked and flaked around his jaw, forcing itself wide as a wet maw pushed up and out his throat.

His groans became a roar, a peculiar one at that, and within a few moments Nick Welsh had succumbed to what he had come to know as the virus, standing face to face to another just like him.

#

If what remained of Nick was still conscious, he would have guessed his son's killer had found him. Had the parasite not consumed nearly all of him, he would have charged. Instead, he snorted and rose on his hind legs, vaguely aware of the vessel he barely had any control over.

The threat lowered its rack, bowed its head as it entered below the retracted garage door. Fire boiled inside of its eyes like flames contained in a glass vile. Worse, it smelled like a reeking combination of blue cheese, warm garlic, and mange. It spoke to him mind to mind, urging him to follow.

Nick curled his lip, no longer wanting to be contained within the three walls of the garage. The beast nodded its rack toward the woods flanking his home, gesticulating its intention.

A yearning to join his counterpart and destroy every living thing crossing their path beckoned fulfillment and the satisfaction it would bring.

The creature lowered, got on all fours, and took its time exiting.

Sean Seebach

What remained of Nick followed.
Inside, his phone rang and went to voicemail.

The Buck Stops Here

#

At seventeen years of age, Jenn Acton got left behind. She followed the convoy through town but got winded and plopped down against an elm tree to rest. Her social media feed was full of posts about a party later that night. But no one had invited her. The best part? She didn't even care. The mystery surrounding the town had become full-on Stranger Things, only without the really cool kids, and she was determined to crack it.

As she caught her breath, a waft of something nasty hit her. She peeked around the elm. Something must have died over in Nick Welsh's garage. Her eyes began to water, and her nose burned. She made a sour face while hitting the camera app on her phone, swiped it to video, and took a few steps forward while tapping record. This could be the break she was hoping for.

I bet there're bodies in there, she thought, inching closer, making faces as her lashes wicked away the moisture from her watering eyes. Then she froze stock-still before dropping to the ground, military crawling toward a bed of wildflowers. Across the street stood a horrifying beast on all fours. Part man, part deer. Two of them since she had shimmied to get a better view, inside Nick Welsh's garage. Strands of mucous gleaming with lines of pink swung like a pendulum from the smaller one. The creature looked infected and was much shorter than the other, frailer even.

While slowly rising between two sunflowers, she angled the face of her phone toward Nick's garage, watching the larger of the two sniffing at the air before vanishing into the woods. Within a few leaps, the second one was gone just as fast. Her heart continued hammering as she checked the footage, confirming she had captured more than just a blurry recording of Nick's front yard.

Chapter 22

"This is bonkers," Dominique said, flipping through Adley's notebook then setting it back on the dash. "I can barely read her handwriting."

"That bad, huh?" Laine said.

"Nah, it's the content that's bothersome."

Laine had her hands at two and ten on the wheel, had hit the emergency lights, and passed all vehicles except for Miss Adley's Buick, which had turned off onto a one lane gravel road before Laine had the chance to take the lead. "You okay?"

"Not really. I got the wife and kids at home and we got a killer on the loose. Monica can shoot though. She's actually a better shot than I am."

Laine felt that. They had abandoned the town they were supposed to protect. But she had gotten used to burying regret, continued telling herself they were doing the right thing here. In an insensitive way, one more person dead was better than a whole slew of people. She couldn't be in two places at once and knew she and Dominique needed to stick together. Power in numbers. Joining Adley and the others in their quest rationalized the decision for her.

As she pulled the cruiser further up a hill, passing the oak sign reading Edward's Escape, Dominique began rubbing his chin. His knee bounced a mile a minute and upon that knee rested his left hand, squeezing his knee as if the sensation would somehow wake him up from this nightmare. Though his eyes were set and focused above set lips, contradicting his own physical behavior.

That gaze shifted toward Laine. "Can I see the photos you took of Chuck? I wanna confirm something."

Laine gestured at her phone mounted to the dashboard and followed Adley's Buick around the driveway's circular design, stopping a good distance away from the cabin while everyone else parked in the sprawling front property rounded by the forest.

Using two fingers, Dominique enlarged a photo and raised Laine's phone. "Look at that."

Laine took the phone and stared at the dead man's feet. The big toe on both were significantly larger than the others. Knuckled and bulging, the digits were an unmistakable flaw in genetics. He removed his phone next. The hoof prints he had taken that morning filled the screen.

"It was Chuck," Dominique said, his face flushing pale. "I thought I noticed it in the basement, but I figured they were all funky from…something else."

Laine compared the two images, eyes dancing back and forth as if watching a ping pong match.

"This shit just got real, Sheriff."

She cleared her throat and nodded.

#

While Miss Adley armed her crossbow, everyone clamored out of pick-ups either via the cab or the bed, in which case they slung themselves over and out, gripping weapons they had supplied themselves.

The cabin at Edward's Escape stood three-stories high, and if it weren't for knowing the true danger which may be inside, she thought it a perfect getaway. A hidden rustic cove came to mind until she saw the divot in the front door. But the divot proved to be a trick of light as twilight settled in. Something had swiped the front door, nearly in two, she noticed while encroaching the covered porch. Half the knocker, a beautiful head of a lion, probably made of brass judging by the tinge of green flecking its face, lay on wide wooden planks.

"It's like something red hot cut right through it." Dominique unholstered his gun.

Behind him stood their support: Bill, Michael, Cody, among others. Even Maggie had a shotgun. Probably kept it behind the bar, Laine thought. An eighth of the town, easy. All set for battle.

Yes, they were a motley group, but they were the heart of Rockbridge and were risking their lives to save it. And they were hers. An overwhelming sense of fellowship filled her at the sight of them before Adley gave a cautious reminder.

"Now this is what I'm talking about, people. And there is no doubt after we slay this dragon we'll all be closer, but I'm afraid it's too late for kumbaya and smores. The parasite has awaken and is starving to eat us all."

Michael held two phones. With one, he snapped photos of the cabin, many of which consisted of the slashed door and the bottom half of the knocker. With the other, he kept locked on Adley as she spoke, probably recording her battle speech. Laine adjusted the PRESS card sticking cockeyed from the band around his fedora. She couldn't help it. It was like licking your thumb and wiping the smudge off a child's cheek.

When Adley was finished, Michael put the phones away and apologetically smiled at Laine, as if he realized she had proven him wrong in some way.

"Damn, you guys smell that?" Big Bad Bill said. "Smells like someone shit their pants and their shit took another shit for good measure."

"It's here," Adley said.

Unarmed, Michael stood behind Laine and Dominique.

All was forgiven. The people of Rockbridge were ready.

Chapter 23

The hunt was on.

Nick's vessel plowed through damp foliage, thorn branches, and rotting logs. His hooves were too keen for the sprawling moss and unbalanced forest ground. He raced at a high rate of speed, keeping pace with the creature leading him. Around him, pulsing light glowed in his peripheral, a green blob here, a violet mass there. He knew he should avoid those colors, many of which could be predators, maybe stop and eat some berries and clover once the colors diminished, but his instincts, at least that of this creature, wanted marrow and tissue. The aroma of blood, pulsing through fresh organs and warm meat filled his nostrils. He drew closer and hurried. Each hoof planted was a stamp, tokens documenting his path of revenge.

His counterpart hinted that the killer was up ahead, and the whole town had come to protect the one responsible. The beast knew no names, and without specifics, convinced Nick to kill them all. Even if they did not possess the smoking gun, Caleb's blood remained on their hands for enabling the murder in the first place.

What the beast communicated seemed as if it was always there. Something not recently learned but known all along.

With the forest whizzing by, Nick had no time to halt. He plunged right into a break in the woods.

Chapter 24

Michael's crotch turned dark the moment he saw the were-deer. Big Bad Bill's chest rose despite the rifle jerking in his trembling hand. Corey had slipped the flamethrower on unnoticed. He glanced in Michael's direction. The guy flared his nostrils, wishing he had it instead of a measly baseball bat. But the bat once belonged to Roberto Clemente (that is what he told people anyway and had gone on to believe it himself) and hoped it had enough magic left to crack another homerun or two.

Lenny held a hunting knife, glanced at it, shrugged, then wielded it while Anthony, no stranger to martial arts, removed a pair of nunchuks from his own back pocket. A spud bar leaned on Dain Stratford's. He used it to size up the two creatures with the five-foot length of steel as if it were a spear.

If you lived in Rockbridge and needed a virus removed from your device or computer, you called Joel Bixby. And if you needed a pickaxe launched at a were-deer, he was also your guy. The pickaxe rested on his shoulder and, of course, a Bluetooth earpiece remained on his ear. But the most impressive of the bunch was Miss Adley, who took a hunter's stance and aimed the crossbow at the bigger of the two.

"Thought there was only one," Bill said.

"Me, too," said Adley.

"Guess you're both wrong," Corey said, yoking the straps of the flamethrower to his chest. He gripped the hose stub and curled his fingers underneath the igniter trigger in one fluid motion. "Let's burn these bitches!"

Laine and Dominique aimed their pistols as the creatures crept on their hind legs, taunting them with their endless horns. The points rose only to twist again in confusing directions. Despite their articulate and deadly design, the were-deer had no issue slithering the many sharpened points toward them.

Their ferocity was masked by their physique, becoming apparent only when the larger one barked. Suddenly, the memory of Squirrel Oliver squatting in the jail cell mimicking the sounds he had heard while hunting rushed back to Laine.

"I expected something more savage than that," Michael said, never at a loss for words.

Even though the bark did not quite match the magnitude of the design, an unease lurked inside of it. If not for the call itself, then in the way in which the beast's tongue fluttered from its horse-like teeth. Chompers big enough to sever a limb. Hooves large enough to slash a bronze door knocker in half.

Or cut someone's head off, Laine thought. And yet, while she stared at the smaller creature, she almost had a sense of pity for it. It remained ten feet behind the alpha, like it was questioning whether it belonged there.

"Adley," she said, "do these things infect others, like werewolves?"

Miss Adley took her eyes off her target for a nanosecond. "I suspect they can. Everyone! Hold your ground! And don't let them bite you. Although I'm afraid they're here for more than a taste."

"Fuck this showdown, bullshit," Corey said. "We're gonna have us a barbecue!"

A stretch of flame shot forward as Corey blasted a ball of fire in the space between him and the were-deer, coating everyone within twenty feet in a blanket of heat. The beasts separated their positions, with the alpha retreating behind the cabin.

"Gotcha cornered, don't I?" Corey confronted the frailer terror, bent his knees, and with a grin squeezed the trigger, but only smoke curled from the end. "This piece of shit already overhea—"

He couldn't finish saying overheated because by that time his lungs had been punctured with a bony, thirty-point rack. Blood shot across the air as Corey's body slung to the dirt.

Dain charged with the spud bar and speared the beta, catapulting himself over the beast in the process. Before he landed, a hoof struck him in the shoulder, followed by another which found his gut. Feces and blood leaked from his lower half while his legs twitched like a fish out of water.

Big Bad Bill fired two consecutive shots, forcing everyone but Laine and Dominique to flinch at the sound. Buckshot spread and continued to fly, directly over the were-deer's antlers. Bill's eyes grew to the size of silver dollars, amazed he had missed such a big target from such a close range. The deer stood on its hind legs and bellowed a comical roar. No one snickered this time, for they had witnessed its capabilities.

Hooves trampled wet grass and Bill turned and ran up on the porch to reload. Dominique and Laine opened fire. Sparks flew from the rack as the creature lowered its head, shielding itself from the onslaught.

The group parted faster than a crowd of people in a room trapping a fart. Laine nearly fell over Michael, who clambered up the steps to get near Bill.

"All right you S.O.B.," Bill said. "This one's for Squirrel!" He took aim as the cabin shook from a sudden crash from inside.

Before Laine could register the source from the ever-growing thudding following the crash, the wall behind Bill exploded, peppering the porch with nails and splinters the size of ice picks. She lowered her gun, paced back, and took a casual glance to her left. For a moment, it seemed Bill wore a mask of the were-deer. From the neck down, he was still Big Bad Bill, operator of B3 Plumbing. Above his shoulders though, writhed the face of the creature. Its maw frothy with mucous and blood, tongue wiggling between its oversize teeth. She did not see where Bill's head landed because a stream of blood flowed over the porch steps and had arrested her attention.

Her gaze lifted upon each step, one by one, and stopped on Michael, whose eyes remained open and staring. The mouth of the blood river was his own. A wooden stake had gone through his ear, pierced through the PRESS card, and tacked it to his head. For the record, the card remained straight as a pencil.

Adley pivoted at a perfect one-eighty and fired. The quills shook long after the arrow pierced the mammoth were-deer's eye. It groaned and thrashed, trampling over Bill's body and crashing through the porch railing.

Dominique wasn't fast enough. He tripped over his own legs trying to flee, falling in slow motion while rapidly clicking the pistol's empty barrel. The hooves left six gaping holes throughout his torso, each one punching clean through.

Laine released her own empty clip and jammed a fresh one in. In a hurry, Maggie lifted her rifle like a tether of rope, hoping to maybe trap the beast's jaws with it but the were-deer bit clean through it, forcing her to drop both halves from the impact. Rapidly, it fluttered its antlers, looking is if they were not moving at all. When they slowed, Maggie's skin peeled from her face like poorly stitched patchwork. She dropped to her knees before the alpha finished her off. One good kick of its rear leg, as if to say good riddance, collapsed her windpipe.

Through the carnage Laine had lost sight of the beta. She noticed Lenny running full tilt with the hunting knife held high as Anthony caused a distraction with his nunchuks, and went to Maggie's side. Now positioned askew from the cabin, Laine could see more of the property, and that was when she saw the beta glance over its shoulder before submerging in the brush.

"I gotta get to the falls, Gail," Adley said, "and burn those parasites. Can you handle this thing?"

Lenny's knife plunged deep into the alpha's muscular hind quarter. For the first time, the were-deer yelped. Anthony approached and undercut the jaw with an upturned swing of the nunchuk. A few of the large teeth fell from its mouth like thawing chunks of ice from an eave. Lenny yanked the knife free and leaped onto the beast. He managed to insert the pointed tip into the neck while avoiding the rack, but eventually lost his grip. As he fell, he seized the handle, creating a twelve-inch incision before landing, before the beast trounced upon his face. The crackle of Lenny's glasses filled Laine's ears, and her stomach turned at the finality of the man's life.

Anthony countered. The chuks landing with every blow, but eventually split down the sides despite their fine craftsmanship. He stood for a moment, dazed, awaiting his fate, and watched the fire in the were-deer's one good eye flicker. Anthony tossed the chuks forward. The chain connected haphazardly, tangling among the points as the bloodied maw opened and the rubbery tongue flapped.

"Oh, God…" Anthony neither whined nor screamed, even with the rack flirting to stab his face with the points of a hundred sharpened knives. The alpha opened wide, but Joel blitzed forward, blindsiding the monstrosity, and swung the pickaxe, burying the point in its spine.

The alpha howled, bucked its head, and Joel rolled forward. He glanced up, blood racing down his bald head. His earpiece flashed.

"Not now, kinda busy," he said, and apparently ended the call. He reached for one of the dangling nunchuks and pulled, hoping to snap them free.

The alpha rose and threw a quick combo, finishing with an uppercut to Anthony's groin as Joel's body split into four pieces, peeling apart one by one like slices from a block of deli cheese. Nothing but a bloody gap remained between Anthony's legs and within that gap hung his lower intestine. He gave the beast the finger as only the whites of his eyes shown and fell like a freshly axed sapling.

Laine reloaded and unleashed into the side of the were-deer, knowing the chase which lay ahead. She did not want Adley going alone, although the woman seemed perfectly capable of handling her business.

The alpha's right side collapsed, finally showing signs of slowing, and toppled over. From where Lennie had made the incision, a cluster of white parasites pulsing with violet burst through the opening and landed in a slimy clump. They twitched among a clear syrup, a substance which smelled of ammonia. Adley wasted no time telling Grant to get his ass over and burn the bastards.

He finally emerged from somewhere between two pick-ups, holding a can of WD-40 and a grill lighter, obviously too scared to fend for himself. Glancing around the carnage, he remained still.

"I snuck over in Lenny's truck bed," Grant said. "Wanted to do the right thing."

"Then get over here and finish this thing!" Adley said.

His shoulders slumped as an uneven gait brought him forward. A frown graced his pallid face. He handed Adley the WD-40 and lighter, then stumbled backward. Laine caught him before he fell and rolled him onto his side. From his lower back bloomed several divots of blood, no doubt the result of friendly fire. Buckshot, to boot. No wonder he had taken shelter. By the time Laine had assessed the cause, his body convulsed. His chest no longer moved. She closed his dead eyes with a swipe of her hand, listening to the makeshift torch behind her burn.

Still crouching, she gazed ahead at the forest. Two crimson orbs glowed in the black of the woods, floating among the trees. Her breath plumed as she stood, reached down, and drove the hunting knife clear across the neck of the were-deer. No other parasites fell out, and the ones that had had shriveled up like black snake fireworks.

Adley removed an arrow from her quiver, placed her boot on the alpha's rib cage, and felt for the heart with the pointed end. The were-deer lay there, chest barely rising, arrow sticking out of one eye, throat slashed, littered with bullet holes, and still, it breathed. Adley put a fast end to that. Using two hands and all her body weight, she thrusted the arrow deep inside the chest.

Slowly, the monster began looking like a normal deer. For a moment, Laine thought, she saw Chuck Edwards's face, a last-ditch effort to maybe confuse her. But she knew where the real Chuck Edwards was, and had a sinking feeling she knew where the real Nick Welsh was too.

Adley slid the quiver off her back. "Won't be needing these anymore." Then she walked over to Corey's body and took the flamethrower. "Glad he left this. This oughta get the entire nest."

Laine stared at the forest, completely unfazed, not even questioning Adley's ability to use it. "One down, two to go."

Chapter 25

Laine kept the beam of her flashlight locked to the path.

They walked for twenty minutes, letting the coolness from the fallen rain which had settled onto the leaves splash their faces. Adley was a courteous neighbor, but her manners had gone out the window once they entered the woods. She paid no mind to the foliage whipping Laine in her wake. But the brisk rainwater kept Laine alert. She didn't mind.

Tracking had never been Laine's strong suit, which is why she had asked Squirrel to accompany her and Chuck in the forest. With darkness settling in, searching for prints would be a lost cause, so she kept her gaze on the two fuel tanks in front of her, allowed Adley plowed forward, and briefly wondering if she would have to kill Adley in order to save Nick.

She really hoped her hunch was wrong and Nick didn't need saving.

As her thoughts drifted to what her life was like only fourteen hours earlier, it was hard for her to imagine what the next ten hours left in the day would bring; along with the days, weeks, and months after. With part of the town slaughtered and both of her officers dead, she decided she would be better off switching careers, maybe move to Ireland or Australia and open her own version of Welsh's Market. Let someone else be responsible for a few hundred people for a change. She had a couple grand laying around in her savings account, but she dipped into it often just to get by. Forty thousand a year salary wasn't much for one person to survive on, let alone uproot to another country and start their own business. She still had fifteen years left on the house too, which needed serious updating if she were to sell.

All of that thinking went under the assumption she would survive the night.

One thing at a time, she thought, and shook the anxiety creeping in from thinking about the required work to fulfill the moment's fantasy.

"Hear that?" Adley said. "Shine your light up a ways."

Laine did and instantly her bladder throbbed. The crisp air combined with the sight of the gushing waterfall up ahead reminded her that she hadn't gone since she left the house. She blew a cloud of breath, noticing the overfill in the pool from which the waterfall fed. Aiming her beam at the rocks, she wondered how Adley planned on getting behind the waterfall when the woman suddenly began tromping around the edges of the pool, navigating over and between mammoth rocks, flamethrower on her back and all.

She glanced down at her own two feet, thankful she had splurged on the eight-inch waterproof boots to accompany her uniform, and followed. Adley began mumbling something, but the roar of the falls drowned her words.

"Miss Adley!"

Adley paced forward, one hand on the stock of the flamethrower, the other outstretched for balance.

"Adley!" Laine sped up. Rocks and slate jutted from where the pool sloped. Mud squished underfoot. Laine nearly fell upon the unfair ground below her. Finally, she grasped Adley's shoulder. She had to shake her for a moment. It seemed her neighbor had fallen under a spell before she faced her.

"What? You just going to rush through the fall and expect to see those worms nestled in a cave?"

Adley's eyes narrowed, then broke their gauge with Laine. "Yes."

Not even a curt nod followed. Adley was that sure.

Laine tugged on her shoulder. "If you're so sure, why didn't you just do it sooner?"

Adley spoke directly into Laine's ear. "Like I said, never had a reason to, until now. Let sleeping dogs lay."

"What if you're wrong? What if there's nothing back there but solid rock?"

Adley looked at Laine's hand, still on her shoulder, and jerked out of the hold. "Then I'll just have to get a jackhammer."

Laine huffed and looked at the sky but saw only stars above arthritic branches. No answers up there. When she dropped her gaze, a flash of red caught her eye. She reached for her pistol, went to plant her foot firmly back, and slipped. Her arms flailed, and in perfect iced-tea-commercial fashion, fell backwards into the pool. The inertia forced her into the chilling depths. Muffled sounds of her struggle to get her body upright flooded her ears. Her eyes were closed, but she knew darkness surrounded her. And in that brackish liquid, if Adley's theory were true, and so far it had been, starving parasites the size of middle fingers on a large hand could tempted to take a nibble at her.

Her hand clawed forward, scraping at mud and pebbles. Even though she had sucked in a good bit of air before she went under, her lungs burned.

Thank God I quit smoking. Air. Breathe. Worms! Four quick thoughts as she kicked her heavy legs which were yet to find purchase, until finally, she got control of herself and swam up instead of over. Her head crested the surface just as her mouth formed a perfect o-shape.

Air had never felt so good entering her lungs. Hand over shoulder, she pedaled her arms to shore and hoisted herself onto the pool's slick bank, bowing her head as rivulets of water ran off her. She unlaced her boots and dumped the water they held. The small amount of make-up she wore clumped between her lashes so she shoved her hand underneath her jacket and dried it off on her khaki work shirt before rubbing the mascara from her eyes. And looked around.

Adley was gone. The two burning holes in the woods remained.

Chapter 26

Laine glanced at the falls, then to the woods, before firing a warning shot. A warning shot only because her bullet went wide right. She was surprised to learn her ammunition had not failed and was relieved to be out of the icy water for more than that reason. Skittering sounds of retreat followed.

She flung her arms, yanked her collar up, and ran her hands through her drenched hair, pinching off the end of her ponytail. A jolt of water shot down the back of her jacket. She did not feel any rubbery, wiggling creatures crawling in her hair or anywhere else after a quick pat.

Adley's boots left deep imprints of their outer soles in the mud. Laine placed her boots overtop those, each one every bit ten inches deep, and winced from the roar of the falls. Water had pooled in her ears. She shook her head from side to side and leaned against the face of the cliff while a frigid mist blanketed her. Yanking her boots out from the final muddy surface of the ground, she hoisted herself onto a stone ridge. Her waterproof flashlight clicked to life.

Sure as shit, a foot away and directly behind the falling water, she had found a cave. It only took a moment to scale the ridge. She focused on her footing, not wanting to ever plunge back into the pool below her. Slices of slate and fine pebbles fell with every step. Biting air scraped across the nape of her neck, practically stiffening her ponytail in place. Strands of it had come loose and lashed at her neck like icy tentacles. She gripped the mouth of the cave and pulled herself inside.

#

Within the flashlight beam fell sporadic drips which landed on the smooth floor patched with moss. Other than the constant ping from the falling moisture, the cave was quiet, and warm. An odor of mildew filled her nose. Laine crouched, bouncing the beam around the walls of the cave which were littered with sigils. They seemed primitive, deeply etched into the stone surface.

She kicked something, then drew her gun, and locked the light to the floor. A skull, yellowed and brittle, rolled toward the shadows. The beam revealed several more skulls, along with skeletal remains long deteriorating from, thankfully, age. She turned, scanning a portrait of a stick figure holding a spear donning an antlered head. Jagged lines surrounded the image.

Worms.

"Miss Adley," she said, barely a whisper, afraid of what she might alarm. "Adley…"

Laine trekked deeper into the cave, thankful the tunnel surrounding her hadn't split into two or three other directions. Because the tunnel wound tightly, she couldn't see more than ten feet ahead, so she listened, keeping her gun gripped in her hand aiming forward.

She expected to hear a blast from the flamethrower by now, but only the trickling water echoed around her. Soon the beam illuminated gems and stone, flashing fleeting shades of blue, purple, and red with every blink of her eyes. Tired from squinting, from attempting to lessen the quality of the glare, she closed them for a moment, afraid to rub them, unsure of the microscopic bacteria and amoebas which may have been living on her sleeve. She had already brought her hand to her face once, a necessary action, but feared overconfidence. This was, after all, uncharted territory, a situation alien to all people except those who had documented their own experiences on the cave's entrance. She took her time, careful not to rush. A single squishy misstep could prove fatal.

The further she went, the more brilliant gems she found. Some were pink, others were turquoise. In any other place, like say maybe a guided tour of some historic cavern, she would have considered the gems alluring and beautiful. But in here, searching for her elderly neighbor who was hunting otherworldly parasites, the gems gave her an ominous feeling. They were the ruse, the innocent person encroaching with their arms outstretched in welcome, concealing explosives underneath their jacket.

Like me, the gems should not be here. This thought forced her to turn around. Only gleaming prismatic color responded. Bending light. She crouched and shielded her brow with her hand. Convinced nothing was following her, she turned back around. A few more feet brought her to another bend in the tunnel. Here, she clicked off her flashlight. Sparkling minerals the size of dimes now flecked the walls. Millions of them. Pressure formed in her head. She popped her ears, listened to the minerals and gems crack below each step, in disbelief of the utter silence blanketing her, when she came to the end of the tunnel.

#

Every end is a new beginning. Where had Laine heard that? Was it plastered across one of the community posters back at the station? She couldn't remember. But if new beginnings were something to hope for, then she hoped the cavern in front of her brought a form of it.

She hopped down the four-foot drop. Her shadow cast long and thin across the den from the array of light behind her. Miss Adley knelt to her left. The flamethrower lay at her side. While rushing to her, Laine flicked on her flashlight. Her shadow instantly retreated.

"You okay?" Laine's boots slopped through muck, accumulating clumps of sludge and pebbles with every step.

Adley didn't respond.

"Miss Adley!" Laine illuminated her, carefully pacing around to face her.

The Buck Stops Here

Adley was stalk still. Pink rimmed her eyes. Red splotches covered her cheeks and neck. Translucent parasites slithered inside the bridge of her puffy nose like a needle threading leather.

Laine's stomach dropped. With a shaky hand, she washed the cavern in white LED light, estimating the size of the cavern to be about two hundred feet in diameter. Her head seemed filled with helium when she noticed a notch in the wall. She narrowed the beam. Atop a mound of clear gelatin writhed pulsing lines of purple and red. A portion of the goop fell from the mass and inched toward her.

She fired a shot, which rang in her ears, something she did not mind at all. Disrupting the quiet reminded her she was fully awake.

The blob imploded, and out from the goop spilled four parasites, each one the size of a beef stick. Laine grabbed the straps of the flamethrower and pulled it behind her as she ran toward her only exit, from where she just dropped. She engaged the trigger and almost dropped the flamethrower's stock. The shear jolt of the flame spitting from the end had startled her.

The parasites quickly shriveled into dust.

She glanced over at Adley, her once sweet, charming neighbor. The woman's mouth fell open. A dry, raspy sound exited her throat. Her hand slowly raised toward the goop atop the slab of slate notched into the wall. An altar.

"I loved you," Laine said to Adley as she drew her gun with her free hand. "May you rest in peace."

Adley's head flung back from the impact of the bullet. Laine washed the woman's body in flames, wishing the silence back. The sound of Adley's skin bubbling and hair frying made her insides somersault.

Without another thought, Laine aimed at the goop. It had stretched itself into a wall, tumbling down then pulling itself up. Flowing, receding. Inside, glowing veins lit up the cavern, illuminating Laine's face in a multitude of color which oddly calmed her.

Sweat beaded her face. Her lip snarled, and she held the ignitor down. All the way. Full blast.

Fire roared like flames from a dragon's throat. The edges of the mass curled, readying to embrace its new host. Laine held the trigger, panning the blaze, lifting it and lowering it as if hosing down a moving van. Within the mass formed acrylic bubbles.

Was the gelatin protecting the parasites?

Laine didn't wait to find out. She released the ignitor and dragged the tank, now much lighter than before, up into the tunnel, now darkened. The once brilliant gems and minerals had an onyx complexion, pulsing with gray. Black as charcoal. Yet, the mass invaded, creeping along at a snail's pace, forming arms which begged to be touched. Laine had the feeling the slightest of contact would be the end of her.

Tank in tow, she flung it at the goop spilling into the air, atop the cavern's ceiling, along the rocky floor. Within the wall of gelatin spiraled the parasites, much larger than the four which had hatched earlier. They corkscrewed from the surface, turning, drilling themselves outward, falling haphazardly, spattering along the mouth of the tunnel.

Laine kicked the stock, shattering several gemstones with the recoil of her boot. Gray dust bloomed around her. She raised her left arm, took two paces back, watching the tank of the flamethrower sink into the goo.

One shot, two shot, three shot, four. She emptied her clip in rapid succession. And ran. She anticipated each curvature of the tunnel, gratuitous of having taken her time through it earlier. The memory of how the tunnel twisted remained fresh in her mind, the muck on her boots providing a decent grip against the floor, propelling her forward. She became aware of the heat following her the moment she leaped from the tunnel and into the cave, where the beta were-deer stood on all fours.

Chapter 27

Laine had no time to engage her last clip of ammo. The notion of being burned alive frightened her more than being speared, trampled, bucked, or even eaten, so she took her chances with the were-deer and focused the flashlight beam into its burning eyes. The beast froze like a deer in…

She plowed forward and hit the creature square in its chest. They spilled out the mouth of the cave and through the waterfall. Laine clutched the antlers at the base and took a deep breath.

#

Full dark set in while Laine was in the cave. Glowing above her, as an exam lamp does in a doctor's chair, floated the moon, full and round. Close enough to the earth that its gray ringed craters were visible. She recalled a sensation of extreme heat following her after firing her gun, which conveniently lay on her stomach. A bolt of pain shot through her neck when she raised her head. She put her hand to her temple and felt something warm, knowing it was blood.

"It'll need stitches."

Laine groaned. Pain wracked her body. Exhaustion set roots in her muscles. Worse, she shivered. But the voice was compassionate, and she knew who it belonged to.

Nick Welsh knelt at her side. His modest position didn't hide the red lashings across his naked body. He gingerly pushed strands of hair away from Abigail's face, exposing the gash above her eye, and rubbed her cheek with a human thumb.

"We nearly sank to the bottom," he said. "You kept a hold of me and I went deeper. Didn't want the fire to get you."

"You're the other one," she said.

Nick looked away.

"How?" she said.

"I was bitten a few weeks ago. Thought it was a rabid animal. Didn't get a good look at it, I guess. Got a rabies vaccine. The wound vanished in a few days. I didn't realize…"

"It infected you anyway."

"I killed my son, Gail. I killed Caleb. I'm sure of it now." His gaze fell. "I would've let the fire take me if it weren't for you hitting your head on the rock when you tackled me."

Nick grabbed the gun and turned it over, almost unsure if it would suffice.

Laine sat up slowly, cringing as she folded her knees underneath herself. "You didn't kill Caleb. Chuck Edwards did. He's the one who bit you. Although, it wasn't really him. The thing overtook him and became its own creature. I know this because of his toe. It was knuckled funny and matched the print we found at the scene."

"I was in the woods the night Caleb was murdered. Adley saw me when I came running out. Didn't think no one would believe her."

He looked far off into the woods. "I didn't even know what I was doing. Doesn't matter anyway, Gail. I'm a monster, but I love you. I hope you will love me back."

"Give me the gun and let's go home. I can prove—"

The gun blast echoed long into the night. Laine gasped. She checked her pockets after blinking for what felt like an eternity. Sure enough, Nick had found her other clip and had loaded the gun, probably while she was still unconscious.

Her body too dehydrated to produce tears, she simply pounded the ground weakly and dry heaved. Nick probably didn't want to go on living without his son anyway. At least, that's what she told herself, and that gave her the courage to pick the gun up and shoot him in the heart. Just to be safe.

"I love you too."

Looking at the permanent smile on his face, she supposed he had made his peace the best he could. She grabbed both of his ankles, brought them to her hips, and dragged him through the woods.

#

Edward's Escape loomed ahead. She pulled Nick's body around the elaborate cabin, past the carnage, and dropped him next to her cruiser before starting it. She glanced at the dead bodies and was too tired to count them all. If one of them came back as a were-deer, she would deal with it when the time came.

She collapsed into the driver's seat and revved the engine, encouraging the vents to blast warm air, and went through the photos on her phone. Sure enough, only one of Charles's toes was crooked and enlarged. She glanced through the window at Nick's feet, confirming only his left toe was protruded awkwardly. Indeed, Charles Edwards had killed Caleb, not Nick Welsh, and knowing Nick had died thinking that he had, brought on a whole new sadness Laine had never felt before. She supposed that's how life went sometimes. You go on thinking about the wrongs you had committed, not even knowing those affected had either long forgotten about them or have already forgiven you. Or, perhaps they were not even that dire in the first place. And without confirmation, those regrets you take to your grave.

The ride back into town was a somber one, full of what ifs and what could have been. And now Laine faced her own future, alone. Her earlier plan of uprooting to another place seemed like a fine idea.

Abigail Laine thought about this when she got home while staring at the cover of Adley's notebook and sipping coffee. She hadn't even changed out of her clothes. Her socks left a trail of brown water on the linoleum, and it would stay there for several days.

The Buck Stops Here

The sun was rising, and she decided she would make the necessary calls after her coffee, give herself time to explain what had happened at Edward's Escape without the mention of bygone parasites and paranormal creatures.

She rose from the kitchen table to get herself another cup, confident in her mostly true account, when her doorbell rang, startling her from thought. She missed the mug while she poured. Hot coffee splashed on her sleeve.

Rather than rolling the sleeve up her arm, Laine simply yanked it up, paying no attention to how uneven the cuff was as she answered the door.

Standing there, with her finger to her mouth, was Jenn Acton nibbling at her lower lip. "Um, Sheriff, I need to show you something." She pointed at her phone. "Can I come in?"

"Of course."

Jenn's voice followed her inside. "I want to first tell you what I saw, then show you what I got, but I doubt you'll believe me."

"Oh, Jenn, I'll believe just about anything right now. Coffee?"

"No, thanks. I was up all night. Coffee's the last thing I need right now."

Laine offered her a seat at the kitchen table while she properly poured one herself.

Jenn sat with her hands folded, phone on the table, watching the steam roll from Laine's coffee mug. She nodded at her arm, the one with the sleeve jerked up. "What happened to your arm?"

Laine's eyebrows formed into two perfect check marks. She sat the mug down. Upon observing her forearm, she noticed teeth marks.

They were crooked.

And she didn't even care.

Printed in Great Britain
by Amazon